APPLE POLISHER

REAR ENTRANCE VIDEO #1

heidi belleau

D1292997

RIPTIDE PUBLISHING

Riptide Publishing
PO Box 6652
Hillsborough, NJ 08844
www.riptidepublishing.com

Apple Polisher (Rear Entrance Video, #1)
Copyright © 2013 by Heidi Belleau

Cover Art by L.C. Chase, lcchase.com/design.htm
Editor: Sarah Frantz
Layout: L.C. Chase, lcchase.com/design.htm

ISBN: 978-1-62649-035-2

First edition
July, 2013

Also available in ebook:
ISBN: 978-1-62649-034-5

APPLE POLISHER

REAR ENTRANCE VIDEO #1

heidi
belleau

RIPTIDE
PUBLISHING

To Bizz, Kristina, Keith, and Ed. You know why.

TABLE of contents

CHAPTER one

AVAILABLE IMMEDIATELY: FULLY FURNISHED
BEDROOM ON THE DRIVE $325/MONTH
HERITAGE HOME
WALKING DISTANCE FROM SKYTRAIN
UTILITIES INCLUDED
HIGH SPEED INTERBUTTS
MUST HAVE GOOD TASTE IN MUSIC
SHARED KITCHEN/BATHROOM
NOT SOMEBODY'S BASEMENT
YOUR OWN ROOM
RAD ROOMMATES—THERE ARE FOUR OF US (ALL GUYS)
YOU EVEN GET A WINDOW
SMOKING OUTSIDE ONLY / NO PETS
DEPOSIT $175
I'M NOT JOKING ABOUT THE MUSIC THING

this is all you can afford now, Christian reminded himself. He folded the ad into quarters, then eighths, stuffed it into his back pocket, and stared at the lopsided house in front of him as if he could turn it into something remotely habitable with the power of his mind.

One of his four possible future roommates (all guys) must be a real estate agent in his spare time, because only a real estate agent could call this dilapidated Edwardian fire hazard a "heritage home." Sure, it was *old* enough to be "heritage," but he didn't know where the "home" fit in unless maybe you were a squatter or a feral cat.

Once-white gables sagged under the weight of a flaking shingled roof, and the yellow paint was a sad shadow of its former cheerfulness: dingy, peeling, and crawling with a film of green moss. What wasn't filthy was in disrepair. It should have been condemned.

Christian made his way up the house's weed-strewn front path, hopped the collapsed first stair of the porch and, left off-balance by his acrobatics, fell into the front door. Hopefully a full-body-and-head knock wouldn't sound any different from the inside than the ordinary with-your-knuckles kind.

"Coming!" someone shouted from inside. "Coming! Coming! Just a second!" And there was a clatter like a class of kindergarteners trampling down the stairs, followed by indistinct yelling. (All guys.)

Nobody answered the door, though, so Christian was left to stand around and scrutinize the stained-glass window above his head. Which could use a few replacement panes, a couple hours of elbow grease, and a bottle or two of glass cleaner. He sighed.

This is all you can afford now, he said to himself again. Maybe he'd get it tattooed on himself, like some people got fortifying tattoos like *This too shall pass*, or *Not all who wander are lost*, or that twee *Lord grant me the strength* poem that somebody had been so kind as to lovingly cross-stitch and hang in a place of prominence on the chemotherapy clinic wall.

At last, a series of clicks came from inside the door, four locks in all from top to bottom: the sign of a house broken into with depressing frequency. Christian stood straighter and tried to wipe the expression of disapproval—*this is all you can afford now*—off his face before the door finally opened a crack.

A round Asian face appeared at shoulder height. "Oh, um, hey," the guy said. "Are you Christian? I mean, Christian the name, not Christian the religion. You're not one of those door-to-door Mormon guys or something?"

"No. I mean, yeah. Christian. From Craigslist. Hi." Christian raised a hand, ostensibly as a wave but mostly to try to convince the nervous-looking kid on the other side of the door that he wasn't armed . . . with a weapon *or* a bible, he supposed.

"Cool, okay. I'm Rob. C'mon in, everybody's in the living room waiting." Without opening the door beyond those first two or three inches, he turned and headed down the hallway.

It went against everything Christian had been taught about manners, but he reached down, grabbed the door handle, pushed—

And the door caught on the chain.

"Oh, sorry," Rob said, and just as he slipped the chain, Christian gave the door another push, sending the door and Christian flying into the foyer—well, not the foyer so much as flat into Rob's face.

Rob stumbled back into the entryway, clutching his nose with both hands and cursing a blue streak that seemed seriously at odds with his previously timid demeanour. Christian, pulling his own hair in sheer panic, followed him in and tried to fit apologies in the spaces between the *fuck*s and *shit*s and *motherfucking cocksuckers*.

"What the hell, man!" yelled someone else, barrelling through a side door and into the already crowded front hall. Two more came in on his heels, which made four. (All guys.)

"It was an accident, I swear!" Christian said, putting his hands up and backing toward the front door.

"It was an accident!" mimicked the last of the four, a short, lanky guy with stretched earlobes and a tattoo creeping out from under his white, ribbed tank top.

This was about to get ugly. This was *all he could afford*, and it was about to get ugly. Might as well give up and drop out of school, work two jobs, and hope he could scrape together enough to pay for a place where he could live alone. Maybe a bachelor suite out in Surrey . . .

But it never did get ugly. Rob stepped between his roommates and Christian, arms out, and said in a small voice, "You guys, it really was an accident. I invited him in and then he pushed the door when I was still undoing the chain and he accidentally hit me with the door. Accidentally. So . . ." He took a deep, fortifying breath, like a man about to make high dive. "So calm your fucking tits, *Max*."

The commotion turned to stunned silence. For a second, all they could do was stand and gawk at Rob, who after his outburst had shrunken in on himself, seemingly waiting for the smackdown. But Max just sniffed, spun on his heel, and disappeared through the same side door he'd initially come through.

"Hit him with the door?" the buff roommate in the popped collar asked, falsely light at first, but quickly regaining confidence again. "You sure we need somebody that accident-prone under *this* roof, Noah?" He slapped the one he'd called Noah on the back, wrapped an arm around his shoulders, and steered him into the door Max had gone through.

Just Christian and Rob left, now. Well, them and the yawning chasm of awkwardness hanging between them.

Christian was about to apologize, but Rob beat him to it. "Sorry about that," he said, rubbing at his elbow and tilting his head so his long dark bangs shadowed his eyes. "Those guys are full of shit mostly. Anyway, um, come on, living room's through here. I guess."

You guess? "Wait, so you still want to interview me? I figured—"

"Nah, it was an accident and they know it. Like I said, full of shit." Rob shrugged, turned, and padded into the living room, leaving Christian in the front hall, bewildered and wondering if it was safe to take off his shoes on the old, splintered hardwood.

He did—mostly because he didn't want to add insult to literal injury and he *really did* need this place—and followed them into the living room. They gave him a place of honour in the room's lone ratty old recliner, leaving everyone else to fight for space on the couch, although currently neither Max nor Rob had taken a seat, so not much fighting was going on. Not about the couch, anyway.

And he *had* gotten a splinter for his trouble. A splinter he was currently forcing himself not to pick at, which took a lot more effort and concentration than you'd think, if the fact that he'd missed at least two-thirds of the current conversation was anything to go by.

As far as Christian could tell, it was Max's fault they hadn't even made introductions or asked him a single question. He and Rob were currently locked in some kind of standoff.

"We all talked it over. We all agreed to do this as a group," Rob said in a distressed-bordering-whiny voice that brought out a tinge of a Chinese accent.

"Yeah, well, that was before he wasted ten minutes pounding your face in. I got a thing to be at. An appointment." Max had his arms crossed over his chest, chin tilted up in some kind of watered-down gangster pose. He kept making aborted motions to edge back toward the door, his brightly coloured tattoo shifting over his muscles.

The other roommates spectated in silence while Rob stubbornly soldiered on, the entire time avoiding eye contact and looking a little like he was going to shake to pieces. "Why would you make an appointment for today? You knew we had to do this. You agreed to it. We all ask him a question. We all vote on whether he gets to stay."

"Fine, fine." Max dug around in the back pocket of his skintight jeans and pulled out a crumpled pink Post-it. He unfolded it, held it about three inches from his face, and read aloud in a voice as shaky as a third grader's, "Who is hot-ter: Megan Fox or Zooey Deschanel?"

Seriously? Max looked at him expectantly. *Yes, apparently.* "I guess I hadn't really . . . noticed."

Max tossed up both arms, the Post-it falling from his hand. "There you have it, boys. My vote's 'no.' Can I go now, *Robert*?"

Rob didn't have a chance to answer; Max had already stormed out.

After a second or two, Noah patted the couch cushion beside him. "C'mon, Rob. He wants to be that way, fuck 'im."

Rob smiled a little and went to take his seat. Noah, meanwhile, turned his blue-eyed gaze on Christian. "Sorry about that. If you still want to live here after all that, we might as well just give you the room here and now. I'm *kidding*, Rob. Anyway, I'm Noah. I'm a sous-chef at an Italian restaurant a couple blocks from here. And this is Rob."

Rob nodded like a dashboard bobblehead. "I'm a first year at Emily Carr." He'd returned to his super-soft speaking voice, his accent smoothing out to a flat—if slightly high-pitched—Canadian one again. "I haven't specialized yet but I'm probably gonna go into sculpture."

The roommate sitting on the other side of Noah, a good-looking muscular guy with a nice tan and a hockey player's wings in his shaggy blond hair, raised a hand. "And I'm Austin. SFU athletics. You go there too, right?"

He'd said as much in his email to Rob, which he now knew had probably been printed out, pored over, and carefully categorized before they'd gotten back to him to schedule this meeting.

"Yeah. Christian Blake. Did a degree in Canadian Studies, now I'm applying for PDP—uh, teaching school. I want to be an elementary teacher."

He could see the *nerd* pass across Austin's features at that. His eyes were already glazing over.

"You doing Kinesiology or Communications?" Christian asked, and Austin gave a good-humoured snort.

"Yeah, you're all right, man," Austin said, sitting back into the sunken couch cushions, and at that harmless familiar barb, the tension vanished from the room. Christian couldn't help but let out a sigh of relief.

They asked him about his personal habits (he showered every day but he was quick about it), his schedule (he was an early riser by necessity but he slept like the dead), whether he had any dietary restrictions (nope), if he had a girlfriend (haha, no), whether he drank or smoked or did any drugs.

"No way. PDP is really strict about that stuff. I've heard of people getting kicked out just for having a picture of them drinking a beer on their Facebook, so I quit all that stuff cold turkey. It's just not worth the risk. Oh, but," he amended quickly, "I don't mind if other people do. I mean, it's cool if you guys smoke weed or have parties or whatever. I'm not judgmental."

That seemed to satisfy Austin, who'd been the one to ask the question.

"So why should we pick you?" Noah asked, very seriously. Christian wondered if he was in charge of hiring the kitchen staff where he worked. "Over anybody else who emailed us, I mean. I'm not trying to freak you out, but we're pretty spoiled for choice here."

Christian jiggled his knee, then forced himself to keep still, reminding himself that this was no worse than the torture of his teaching school interview. Not to mention fidgeting made the whole couch shake.

Because this is all I can afford, that familiar nagging voice in his head supplied, *and I don't have anybody left I can depend on and I don't know how I'm going to afford these tuition payments coming up and I don't know if this scholarship money is going to come through and—*

"I always do the dishes?" he tried.

"Sold!" Austin laughed. "Rob? Noah?"

Rob, who'd been mostly mute during questioning, brushed his hair back over one ear. "It would be nice to have some help cleaning up after dinner . . ." he murmured.

They all turned to Noah. Noah, who had explained earlier how he owned the house after inheriting it from his great-uncle but preferred for things to be democratic rather than having to act as a landlord. Which, of course, was a nice sentiment, but when your name was on the deed, it meant diddly-squat. "Yeah, okay," he said. "So that's three to one. I guess you're in, Christian. Rob'll show you your room, give you the big tour of the house, and if you like what you see he'll get your deposit and give you your key. Anything else you wanna say before we get going?"

Yeah. I'm gay. That's part of why I'm in this fucking mess. But don't worry, I'm too terrified of getting kicked out of teaching school to dare get laid.

He took a deep breath. "Yeah, just one question. Aren't you gonna ask me about my taste in music? Or was that one of Max's hard-hitting questions?" He grinned, baring his teeth.

"It was me, actually," Rob admitted. Half a smile tugged at his pouty mouth. "The last guy who had your room was some weeaboo into J-pop and if I heard Smile.dk one more time I was gonna throw his laptop out a window."

He moved in the next day.

The hostel had been a lifesaver after his abrupt departure from SFU's suddenly overpriced campus residence, but that didn't mean he wasn't happy to leave. No more worrying about his miserable roommate's inexplicable mood swings and casual racism. No more smelly backpackers. No more acoustic guitars. No more carrying his valuables wherever he went, even to the shower.

He wasn't sure about Max, but the other guys in his new "heritage home" seemed pretty aboveboard. He'd learned on Rob's tour that his bedroom even had a lock, something you didn't really appreciate until suddenly you were without one and some racist asshole was free to riffle through your stuff every time your back was turned.

So yeah. A lock. The latest in a series of small-but-welcome reliefs that the last few months had taught Christian to appreciate. Only Noah and Christian would have a key, as was house policy, and Rob had been quick to assure him that Noah never abused his not-landlord privileges. Even so, Christian would give it a couple weeks, feel them all out, and maybe then decide how paranoid he needed to be.

Not that he had anything worth stealing anymore, not after he'd sold off all of his non-essential electronics to keep him afloat through to the end of last semester. In fact, he didn't own much of anything *period*, worth stealing or not. So he arrived on the doorstep in the morning with an overstuffed hiker's pack, the clothes on his back, and a laptop under his arm. That was it. His entire life.

His aunt would tell him life was more than "things," in that voice-of-experience way that he couldn't dare fight with, but she wasn't here, and his basic sanity demanded that he not think about her too hard or too often. Heartless, but necessary, what with the spectre of his gruelling back-to-back practicum semesters looming. He needed to focus. She understood.

Rob met him at the door.

"Oh!" he said, and then bit his lip, casting his gaze across the porch. "Is that everything you have? Is there more coming? I thought I'd help you move in. I mean, if you want. Me. To help you."

Christian had to wonder what Rob would have done if he *had* needed help with his stuff. Not that Christian was a linebacker or anything, but Rob had to be a hundred and thirty pounds soaking wet. But he obviously liked to be useful, so Christian handed him the laptop with what he hoped was a grateful smile. "Yeah, I'm kind of a nomad. Don't own a lot of stuff."

Rob also seemed keen to play the role of host, so Christian allowed himself to be led to his own room. "I cleaned it myself after the last guy moved out," Rob said, hugging the laptop to his chest as he waited for Christian to unlock his door. "Top to bottom. A year's worth of Pocky crumbs. Can't say the bathroom or kitchen will be even half as clean, sorry."

"Don't be." Christian tossed his bag onto the bed, put his hands on his hips, and surveyed his new room. *His.* Despite how decrepit it was, he still felt the same high he'd felt when he'd first moved into residence four years ago. He wondered if being out from under his mother's watchful eye would ever get old. He squinted at Rob. "Hey, how come you live here and not in the dorms? Or with your parents, even? They not live in the lower mainland?"

The question obviously took Rob by surprise, because he gaped like a fish. "Dorms are too expensive, as I'm sure you know. And I may not look it but I *am* of age. It's not like I'm some sixteen-year-old art prodigy. My parents are just out in Coquitlam. I told them I didn't want to make the commute, but mostly I needed to get out of there, you know?"

Christian shrugged, the question cutting him too close.

"They're really good parents. It's not that kind of thing where they want me to be a doctor or a dentist or something. They're even paying my tuition and part of my rent here. They're totally supportive, I mean. It's just . . . It's not . . . It's not them, it's me."

Well, that was weirdly defensive. "Oookay." Christian pointedly turned and unzipped his bag, hoping Rob would take the hint.

He didn't. "What about you?"

"My mom's back in Jamaica. I have an auntie here, but I only met her after high school so I'd feel weird moving in now. That and she has other stuff on her plate."

Other stuff. That was one way to put it. Ovarian cancer. Other stuff.

"Back in Jamaica? *Back*? Are you from Jamaica?"

Was he going to have to tell the kid his whole life story?

No. That wasn't fair. Rob sounded genuinely interested, and he hadn't done anything to deserve the cold shoulder. If Christian was going to become a teacher, especially teaching little kids, he needed to learn to be cooler about personal questions. "No, I was born here. My mom's from there though. She moved back when I was seventeen."

"Are your parents divorced? Did you stay with your dad after that? That must have been hard."

Be nice, a voice urged him. He didn't know if it was his inner teacher, or his aunt.

"Yeah—"

Max's head popped out from behind the half-closed door. "Knock knock! Oh hey, nugget!" he greeted Rob, then nodded solemnly to Christian. "New Guy."

Christian nodded back.

"Just back from a run." Which explained why he was a little breathless, his short curly hair sticking damply to his forehead. A flush of exertion covered both cheeks and followed the line of his nose up to his forehead, and a sheen of sweat hung on his upper lip until he somewhat licked it away. His tongue was pierced. Oh yes, Christian noticed, although he had the good sense to hate himself for it. "It's hot as the devil's ball sac out there. I, uh . . . I drank that bottle of water you had in the fridge." He flashed Rob a not-nearly-apologetic-enough look.

Rob's hands balled up into fists. "The Fiji bottle? The one with the Post-it that said 'ROB'S, MAX DO NOT DRINK'? That one?"

"Oh, I didn't see a Post-it. It was probably the condensation on the bottle, it probably washed the glue off. You know how it is with condensation."

"How *convenient*."

"Aw, don't be like that. You know I'm good for it. I'll have some cash Friday night. I'll buy you a whole case." He was laying on the charm real thick, smiling like a wolf. *The better to eat you with.* "You still love me, right?"

"Hmmph," Rob replied, but the corner of his lip twitched in a smile nonetheless.

God, was there something going on between them? Had he unwittingly walked into Noah Hadley's House for Wayward Gay Boys?

No way.

CHAPTER two

m ax made good on his promise. Friday morning, Christian stumbled down to the kitchen, threw open the small shared fridge, and discovered that an entire shelf had been swallowed up by a flat of Fiji water, labeled with a Post-it that said simply, "Rob."

In fact, Max seemed to have a whole shitload of money to splash around. That evening he bought them all beer, an obscene amount of pizza, and a new Xbox game to play while they ate. He wouldn't take repayment for any of it, either, not even from Christian, who barely knew him.

Barely knew any of them, actually. The wildly diverging sleep schedules and shifts for their various jobs didn't leave much time for socializing, and even if it did, Christian had found it hard to leave his room much over the last week. He spent his time split between looking up lesson planning on the Comic Sans-riddled corner of the internet where teachers dwelled, and scrolling through WebMD and way more sketchy "natural health" websites than he cared to admit.

So the Friday night pizza and first-person shooter-fest seemed like a cosmic sign. A stop-looking-at-websites-that-blame-cancer-on-fluoride kinda sign. A Jake-Bass-will-never-sleep-with-you-so-meet-a-real-guy-already sign. Okay, maybe not the last one. Teaching school. Closet. Celibacy. Right.

Living in a house full of hot mid-twenties guys *really* wasn't helping on that front. Ever since Christian had come out (only to head right back into the closet again, but never mind that), he'd spent at least half his time trying to convince people that the whole predatory-gay thing was about as true as the you-can-get-AIDS-from-a-toilet-seat thing and just as offensive. But the combination of no sex and Noah Hadley's Home for Wayward Gay Boys was turning him into a walking stereotype with an unruly boner.

He couldn't help but take an inventory, now that they were all in the room together.

Item one: Noah Hadley himself, now seated in his recliner and devouring his third slice of pepperoni pizza. Tall, kinda tubby, blue eyed, brown haired, perfectly average looking except for how he grew the kinda scruff you desperately needed to drag your fingernails through, that made you think he just had to have a gorgeous bush, too. And all that focus on knife work for his job, he had to be good with his hands.

Item two: Austin Puett, the second youngest in the house at twenty-one, sitting on the couch next to Christian with a slice of pizza hanging out of his mouth by the crust and a controller in his hands. Muscular. No, work-out-five-times-a-week muscular. Goofy smile, like an eternal teenager. Buckets of dumb jock appeal. Bad cologne, but nothing a hot shower (together) couldn't fix.

Item three: Rob(ert) Ng, on the floor at Noah's feet, legs stretched out in front of him and still painstakingly picking mushrooms off his first slice of deluxe. The youngest guy in the house, and the most earnestly awkward, too. Not exactly Christian's type, but for a certain set, he'd be a real prize: slim, as slightly built as a fashion model, and a pout that could get him anything, just so long as he asked the right guy. No wonder he hated weeaboos so much. They probably treated him like a demigod . . . just so long as he played the role *they* wanted him to.

Christian knew that feeling, except in his case they all wanted him to play the thug and were sorely disappointed when they got mild-mannered kindergarten teacher instead.

And then there was Max.

Christian swung his eyes to the television, the screen bisected for two players, and then down to the slice of pizza hanging limp in his hands. Anywhere but—

—Max. Item four. No last name. Not even Noah knew it, or if he did, he was keeping it real hush-hush. Compact and wiry, dark curly hair, full lips, Roman nose. A few freckles on his high cheekbones. Big hands with knobby knuckles. Somewhat badly dressed in skinny jeans and ironic thick-framed glasses that ten-to-one odds weren't prescription. Still owned a skateboard in 2013, and somehow that made him all the more appealing. And the tongue piercing. Couldn't forget the tongue piercing.

Clearly Christian should have gotten over his bad-boy stage in high school like everyone else did, because this was just *painful*.

Of course, then Max would open his mouth, this time yelling "Get some!" at the screen, and Christian would be cured again. Thus released, he ate his free pizza with gusto, punched Austin in the shoulder when Christian's turn with the controller set the jock off shit-talking, and refused at least five offers of free beer, even though the temptation was nearly destroying him.

Nobody asked Max where the money had come from. And after a week of Mr. Noodles, and still on unsure footing with all of his roommates but puppy-dog Rob, Christian wasn't about to rock the boat.

That night, Christian went to bed with a belly full of pizza, but still *hungry*. Jake Bass would have to suffice.

The restlessness didn't last long. There just wasn't time for it.

The following Monday was the start of classes on campus, nine-to-five days spent going over classroom management plans and grading procedures and ethics workshops and arguing in circles about standardized testing. A semester and a half of this, and then he would finally be assigned to an actual public school classroom and be taking on actual student teaching duties. Marking. Teaching. Photocopying. More photocopying. More marking. The thought of his student teaching practicum was simultaneously a dream and an absolute nightmare. And did he mention no pay for any of it?

His first week ended with a long lecture on professional appearance and how they were expected to dress the same on campus as they would in their practicum classroom. Which meant no sneakers, no ripped jeans, no T-shirts, and "A tie wouldn't be remiss, either," his professor concluded.

That was how Christian found himself trawling every thrift store he could find that Friday, searching for a suitably "professional" new wardrobe among the racks of ratty old men's jackets and threadbare golf shirts before finally giving in and heading to a department store instead, where he spent money he didn't have—well, money he *did* have, but was supposed to be for groceries—on clothes he didn't want.

"Mall madness?" asked Max as Christian collapsed into Noah's recliner, arms weighed down with bags full of overpriced pressed slacks and respectable button-downs.

"Something like that," Christian replied, not willing to get into it over such a toothless barb, although he could have just as easily said, *Some of us work for a living.*

Max was lounging around, looking not even the remotest bit "respectable" and enjoying every minute of it, damn him. Sprawled across the couch like he was about to ask someone to "Draw me like one of your French girls," he was wearing a poppy red pair of skinny jeans with black high-top Chucks (never mind Rob's rules against shoes in the house) and a black V-necked T-shirt that showed off the lean muscles of his arms and the upper left corner of the vibrantly coloured tattoo over his heart.

"Actually . . ." Christian said, latching onto fleeting inspiration, "It's for work. Well, school. School. Work. School."

Max raised an eyebrow, and Christian could *sense* the smug amusement at his flailing.

"You know how it is." He paused for effect. "*Don't you?*" It wasn't as elegant as it had sounded in his head, but he'd still, in his roundabout way, put it out there. Confronted Max with the question, without actually saying it: *What the hell do you even do?*

Last week he'd paid for those pizzas. That flat of expensive water. Even the clothes on his back. Rent, of course. He had to get that money somewhere, and the fact that he wasn't upfront about it like a normal person was driving Christian *insane.*

"Not really," Max replied, a shrug in his voice, and reached down to scratch his flat belly just above the waistline of his jeans.

Damn you, you shameless, smooth-talking bastard.

The scratching turned into an absentminded stroke, drifting fingers lifting the hem of his top to expose an inch or so of skin. An inch or so of skin bisected by a narrow line of dark hair.

Christian looked away.

"So all those clothes . . ." Max ventured, "they're for that teaching thing you're doing, right?"

It was the first time they'd actually *talked*. Christian felt kind of guilty for using it as an opportunity to twist the guy's arm for information.

"Yeah. I knew I was going to have to buy that stuff anyway—they hold student teachers to completely different standards than the actual professionals, and to be honest it's kind of *bullshit*, like why do I have to wear a tie when the guy I'm sharing a classroom with is wearing a T-shirt and fucking flip-flops—but, uh . . ."

Max raised an eyebrow, obviously trying not to smile.

"But not so soon. I figured I had six months before my practicum started, but no, apparently we don't just have to dress like this when we're teaching, we have to dress like it all the fucking time. Kind of a culture shock after undergrad, when you could roll out of bed and go to lecture in your pyjama pants and a Che Guevara T-shirt, you know?"

An awkward laugh. "Uh, not really, man. I dropped out of high school. Couldn't stand to stay in one place long enough to do the whole school thing. I got my GED, but that's it."

"Oh. Well, um . . ."

"But I still know who Che is, so don't think I'm some fucking idiot."

"Got it."

They sat in silence for a while, Christian trying to come up with a convenient excuse to leave. He had to make a phone call? He needed to take a shit? He was late for a webcam session with a potential mail-order bride?

Was there a reason most of his excuses seemed desperate to establish him as straight?

"Why do you do that, man? I couldn't." Max rolled onto his side, eyeing Christian from over the arm of the couch. He was hugging himself, a gesture Christian read as self-conscious, except that didn't make sense.

"Do what?"

"Do a job that wants to change who you are."

"Wh-what? What do you mean by that? I mean, it doesn't? It doesn't. Does it?"

"You can't drink. You can't smoke weed. Now you can't even wear your own clothes. Is it worth it?" His dark eyes were fathomless, patient and expectant and *oh God was he actually being serious here? Was he asking a serious question?*

Christian wasn't prepared for the possibility of that. Glib douchebaggery, he could handle. Could even brush off with a joke. But not this. "Can't swear, either," he answered, out of some strange desire to up the ante on Max's assessment of the situation. "And if you think what you drink or smoke or wear makes you who you are, that's pretty sad."

Max sat up straight, levelling at Christian the same serious look, except tempered this time by anger. "And *I* think it's sad that *you* don't get the fact that the clothes are just the tip of the iceberg, here. If they think they have the right to control that, then what else— You know what? *Whatever.* Forget it."

He got up. Strode out of the living room without another word.

Christian was left sitting bewildered on the couch, trying to wrap his head around Max's outburst. And the question Christian hadn't answered.

Is it worth it?

Of course it was!

Christian scrubbed at his head furiously, staring down at the shower taps as if they were Max's smug under-achieving face.

Because while you and every other normal boy were out playing soldiers and cops 'n' robbers and pee-firemen, I was downstairs in my mother's basement, using the walls as a chalkboard to teach every girl in the neighbourhood how to do their letters and making them all raise their hands to speak. And okay, maybe that sounds like a power trip, and maybe it was *a power trip, but it's not anymore. It's so much* more.

Something worth the sacrifices he'd made, and not just the clothes and the booze and all the other millions of ways he found himself editing himself, trying to cultivate a life and a public image that was suitably untouchable for a teacher. The money. The time. The sheer fucking effort.

And they are sacrifices, *Max. As in, things I give up willingly to achieve my dreams. Not that you know anything about that.*

He ducked under the shower, half to wash the shampoo out, and half to cool his fucking head. (Because what started as a hot shower never ended as one in this goddamn house, but that was beside the point right now.)

Sacrifices. Not *things taken away from me.*

God. Get over *it, Christian.*

Three days, and he was still rehearsing speeches and coming up with (not so) scathing comebacks. *Three days!*

He should have been focused on his studies—after all, he had a practice grading rubric to create by Friday that he hadn't even looked at—or maybe on some creative ways to make some quick cash before all this ramen he was eating killed him from malnutrition. And then, if he *still* had spare time after all that, he could obsess a bit more about how truly fucked up his personal life was becoming. His aunt. Okay, his aunt's *illness.* His mother, even, and the horrible evil thoughts he'd been having lately of contacting her and making his return to the closet a permanent thing.

But no. That would be too far. It was one thing to pretend for a class of students and their parents to be a person devoid of sexual desire, and maybe once he was comfortable (read: tenured) settle down with a "roommate," but bringing his mother into it would be to give up entirely. Live a *real* lie.

He wondered what Max would think of that.

Man, fuck Max.

That small wiry body bent forward on Christian's bed, ass up and know-it-all mouth buried in the sheets. Christian buried—

No! Don't fuck Max! Don't fuck Max at all!

Christian already had his half-hard cock in his hand, and now he was staring at it like it was some kind of treacherous alien thing. Okay, so the celibacy plan wasn't working out too great. A guy had to let the pressure off somehow. He was a teacher, not a saint.

But God, *anybody* but Max. Bad enough to have the hots for any of his roommates—it seemed like a handwritten invitation for all manner of drama and awkwardness, especially since he still didn't intend on coming out to any of them—but *Max?* At least Austin was clean-cut, a fellow student with just as much reason (theoretically, of course) to keep it in the closet. At least Noah had a steady job with an explainable income to match. And even though he didn't have the vaguest physical attraction to him, at least Rob seemed too socially stunted to do anything other than pine away.

Max was a fucking *minefield*.

A sexy, mysterious, bad-boy minefield with great arms and tight jeans that left very little to the imagination.

Christian groaned in defeat, bracing himself against the grimy tiled wall with one hand while the other got on with the shameful business of manhandling his dick.

"Nobody has to know," he said aloud, surprised to hear himself panting already. After all, as guilty as he felt, he *was* alone in a locked bathroom, and none of his roommates read minds. He could do this, wash his hands of it (literally and figuratively, um), and forget about it. Yes. That.

He fell head-first into the fantasy. Pounding into Max from behind, squeezing his ass and thighs, biting those arms, turning him over and licking and sucking on his nipples. Kissing him.

Kissing him?

Christian shook the thought out of his head and gave himself a punishing squeeze, which tragically backfired since it served only to make him buck into his own hand for more.

Not kissing, he thought to himself sternly, keeping up the rough pace. Just fucking. Max wasn't the type of guy you held hands and cuddled and kissed with. You fucked him. You sucked him. Yes.

Mmm, or maybe *he* sucked *you*. Max's full lips wrapped around the shaft of his cock, so plush and fucking luxurious . . . *Yes, yes.*

His conscious mind resurfaced. He'd covered the front wall of the shower in cum. There were even a few drops on the taps. But God, he felt good. Sated. The first time he'd felt just . . . *satisfied* in a long time. He shuddered through an aftershock, eyes rolling back in his head with the sheer decadent pleasure of it.

And then somebody knocked on the door.

"Christian?" Rob's small voice called through the door. "Christian? Are you almost done in there?"

Fuck!

Christian slapped at the shower stream, trying to splash the evidence of his undoing off the wall. "Yeah, um, yeah, just a second, coming!" *Oh, bad choice of words.* "Just uh . . . just washing the shampoo out of my hair?"

Out, damned spot!

Splashing was no use. He reached down, wiping the tiles with his bare hands, smothering the urge to gag. *Pretend it's shampoo. Yeah. Shampoo. Nothing wrong with getting that on your hands.*

"Okay . . ." Rob was apparently content to wait right outside the door until Christian finished. Awkward little fuck. What should have taken thirty seconds suddenly felt like it was taking hours. "Well, uh, I kind of accidentally answered your phone because you left it in the kitchen and it was ringing off the hook and uh—sorry? But it's your aunt calling. Do you want me to tell her you'll call her back?"

"No!" Christian shouted. He yanked the taps closed and leapt from the tub, knowing full well he hadn't finished cleaning his mess and just plain not caring, just the same as he didn't care right now that Rob had been presumptuous enough to answer his cell. "No! No! Coming! Coming now!" He threw a towel around his hips and fell out the bathroom door, snatching his cell from Rob's hand.

"Auntie," he greeted, breezing past Rob and into his room without a word of thanks or reproval for taking his call. He slammed the door shut behind him. Locked it. "How are you doing? Everything okay?"

She laughed. "Your hair grey yet, Christian?"

He knew she was joking, but he still turned to his bedroom mirror and prodded at the mess of wet curls that was quickly rising into its usual cloud around his head. "No, Auntie," he replied.

"Do you *want* grey hair?"

"No."

"Then slow down, *bwoy.*"

"Sorry."

"I haven't talked to you in weeks. How you been?"

He sighed in relief. Ever since she'd first told him over the phone about her cancer, every single call from her gave him the same feelings of anxiety. He was always expecting bad news. The worst news, if that were even possible.

But no, she'd just called to talk. Of course she had. He hadn't put out the effort to call her in weeks, and wasn't that just bullshit, after he'd promised himself to never take another moment with her for granted?

"I've been busy with school— *No.* No excuses. I'm sorry, Auntie. Yeah, I'm busy, but I should *make* time."

"Yes, you should. But stop the flagellation. Tell me about school. You changed your mind about being a teacher yet?"

She always joked like that, saying no reality of teaching could ever live up to his fantasies of saving the world one kid and one report card at a time. That he'd get burnt out when it wasn't all *Dead Poets Society* and *once you realize it, you can come work for me*. She was just teasing, of course. She knew how much this mattered to him, even though she didn't understand it. To her, nothing was worth compromising her strange, glorious self. When it came to the ties argument, she and Max would definitely be on the same side.

That was why he loved her. That screw-the-naysayers, be-who-you-are worldview, as inconvenient as it was now, had saved his life, once. Not just his physical life. His soul.

Was he really going to throw all that away with this back-into-the-closet experiment?

"Nope," he replied, finally. "But they got me wearing a tie and trying not to use slang. I don't know how much longer I'm gonna last."

"You'll last right through to the end and you know it. Stubborn goat."

For a while after that, they just talked like old times while Christian towelled his hair. He told her about his new place, smoothing over some of the more unsavoury aspects of the structural integrity of the house. Told her about his roommates, but briskly changed the subject when she asked if he was sweet on any of them. And then, when they'd gotten past all the juicier gossip, he told her about school. The assignments. His fears about his practicum.

"Did your student loan come through all right?" she asked.

Christian's heart dropped into his stomach. It should have been an innocuous question. With anybody else, it would be.

But not with her.

"Auntie, do you need to tell me something? No, never mind. I'm gonna come see you. Right now. You at home?"

"No, no, don't come see me. You have homework. Way too much on your plate. How about you come around on Saturday instead and I take you out to lunch?"

"Nope, not an option. I'm putting on my shoes right now." He wasn't, of course. He was still in his towel, actually. But she didn't know that. "You can't convince me not to come, so you better just tell me. Are you at home?"

"Yes, yes," she sighed.

All through his BA, she'd been the one to foot the bill. *Happy to*, she'd said. *What else is family for?* Every bill, she wrote him a check. Tuition. Room and board. Books. Bus passes. Athletic fees. Every single cent of it came out of her pocket.

Until suddenly it didn't.

A few months back, nearing the end of his last semester of undergrad, she'd called and asked him how he was doing for money. Whether he'd gotten any scholarships. Were his res fees all paid up. Finally, after dancing around the issue for as long as possible, she'd admitted to not having the money to give him a full ride anymore. It wasn't the money that made her so ashamed, it was why she didn't have it.

Because she was sick.

CHAPTER three

auntie Beverly lived in a shoebox masquerading as a condo down near Davie Street, smack in the middle of the village. Her roommate, a middle-aged, white lesbian named Sandra, had the nastiest temper Christian had ever seen, so he only very rarely stopped by there, preferring to meet his aunt on neutral ground in nearby restaurants.

But he'd had more important things to think about than Sandra when he'd had his aunt on the phone, so enemy territory it was. Aunt Beverly met him at the door, accepting his extended offering of a used paperback with a good-natured kiss on the cheek.

He always brought her gifts, whatever he could afford. But since he was too old to make macaroni art, a copy of *The Da Vinci Code*—bought for fifty cents from a hippie selling his wares off a blanket on the sidewalk—would have to suffice. It was a far cry from the bottles of wine and bouquets of fresh-cut flowers and even boxes of mandarin oranges he used to bring by back when he was working part time, but she seemed just as thankful for it.

She looked . . . okay. Still too thin, which for her meant too big to wear Lululemon, but her own clothes hung on her. The red and purple scarf she wore tied around her head was cheerful enough, though, and so was her tone of voice.

"You look sharp!" she said as they went together into her small kitchen. Her condo had a breakfast nook surrounded by bright full-length windows, the little table there smothered by stacks of receipts and invoices and red-inked employee schedules.

Christian took a seat in one of the chairs not taken up by Bankers Boxes while she put a kettle on. "Thanks. It's this new professor. He wants us to wear business casual to classes and I figured I might as well just do it full time. You know, so I can get used to it." He tugged at the buttoned collar of his shirt in illustration with a smile.

Which wasn't even remotely true, of course. He hoped the nice clothes gave her the illusion that he was doing decently well for himself. Not like she could tell by looking at him that he'd bought them with his grocery money, right? It was just that she had this bad habit of throwing money at him, even after she'd said she didn't have any to spare.

"How's the store?" he asked, because he wasn't ready to ask, *How sick are you?*

She heaved a big sigh. "Not so good." She wouldn't look at him as she said it, just busied herself getting out mugs and tea bags.

"'Not so good' as in about the same as it's been for the past few months"—*since you got sick*—"or 'not so good' as in worse?"

"The second one," she admitted. She came to the table with their mugs, setting a cup of black tea down in front of him. She removed a stack of papers from another chair and sat herself down before looking at her tea and startling. "Oh, shoot." She looked on the verge of tears.

"Honey?" Christian asked, already on his feet.

"Yes, please."

He wondered if maybe he shouldn't have asked if she wanted him to move in. Take care of her. Maybe he could ask now. He didn't have a lease with Noah, after all. He could postpone school. Not like he could afford it, anyway. *No.* She'd take it badly. So he brought her the honey instead, sat quietly while she added two huge globby tablespoonsful.

"I'm thinking of just selling," she said, blowing on her tea, still not meeting his eyes.

"No!" She couldn't. That store, as freaky and kind of gross as it was, was her baby. Her pet project. Her second (maybe even first) home. It would be like Christian giving up teaching. The cancer had taken her hair, taken her time and money and well-being. It couldn't take her business, too. It couldn't.

"*Yes*," a third voice said. Christian looked over to the main kitchen area, and of course it was Sandra, standing at the counter and pouring a third cup of tea. Even in a sports bra and yoga pants, the woman was absolutely terrifying. With her blonde hair pulled back in a ponytail, her face was as sharp as a stiletto, all feminine angles and I-will-step-on-your-balls intensity. "And is it a wonder, what with her hero nephew who can't even be bothered to stop by and visit, let alone help out?"

Christian shrivelled under her gaze. "I try to come by when I can," he mumbled. "Here now, aren't I?"

"Oh, yeah? And where were you last week when she had a doctor's appointment and would have had to take the bus alone if *I* hadn't driven her?"

"Sandy, that's not fair," his aunt said, but she didn't sound angry at all. "He's in school. He can't give that up to come take care of me."

"Oh yeah? Why not? What could he possibly be doing that's so damn important?"

What indeed.

Auntie Beverly took a slow sip of her tea, her dark eyes peering at Sandra from over the mug. They were kinder, but just as sharp as Sandra's. "That's not the point and you know it. I don't *want* him to give up school. I don't want *anyone* to put their life on hold for my sake, including you."

Sandra sniffed. "Well, I'm happy to do it anyway."

"So am I!" Christian put in. *Even though I haven't done anything to prove it.*

"Yeah? Then how come that store is such a mess? How come she has nobody to cover her shifts? How come she doesn't have anybody to do inventory and get her stock in?" It wasn't the speech of a woman talking out of her ass. Beverly had obviously been complaining to her, worrying to her, confiding in her. And for Auntie Beverly to complain to anyone about anything like that . . .

"Is the store really in that much trouble?" Christian asked.

"She's exaggerating," Auntie Beverly said softly, and Christian knew it was a lie.

"No, I'm not." Sandra slammed her mug down on the counter. "If you were around more, Christian, you'd know I'm not."

"I'm still paying my staff." Beverly wasn't even looking at them now. God, she looked so *tired*. It was breaking Christian's heart.

"Yeah, and how long can you keep that up? Tell him the truth, Bev. He's a grown-ass man."

Beverly drummed her purple nails up and down the sides of her mug. Up. Down. Up. Down. "We've . . . we've got at least a couple thousand dollars in unpaid late fees we can collect that nobody has the time to chase down right now. We get those in, then maybe . . ."

"Then maybe what, you stay afloat another couple months?"

Jeez, Sandra was being so hard on her. Christian didn't mind being chewed out (and really, he did deserve it), but to see Sandra turn that same fury on his aunt . . . "C'mon, lay off her. She's doing her best. She'll pull through, you'll see. She'll get those late fees in, she'll hire someone new, the place'll get restocked, the customers will follow. If you build it, they will come, right? Maybe she can't work eighty-hour weeks anymore, but—"

"I can't work at all." Beverly's voice was clear, determined. Final. Christian went silent, all his optimism draining out of him at once. Even Sandra's face softened from her usual anger into pained sadness. "I . . . I'm not allowed to go back. I'm sorry, Christian, I should have just told you upfront. It's my white cell count. It's too low. Doctor says I can't risk an infection. Can't be around customers, even if we only see ten of 'em a day. They're stopping the chemo, too. They're hoping if I take a break from treatments, take some supplements, then maybe . . ." Her voice got weaker and weaker until it trailed off into tears.

Sandra started, but Christian was faster. He stood, walked stiffly around the table, and pulled his aunt against him in a tight hug. His heart pounded in his chest, thumping so hard he thought maybe he was going to pass out, but he didn't. She was so short, and he was so tall, that sitting in a chair, her head was barely higher than his navel. *So small.*

He bent down and rubbed her back, holding his breath as he did so, afraid to smell her. The smell was the worst part—not because it was particularly unpleasant (in fact, it was more sweet than anything), but because it just served to remind him that something fundamental inside her had *changed*, something that touched every part of her even when she otherwise seemed okay.

"You'll figure it out, Auntie," he said, secretly giving Sandra a censorious look over his aunt's head, just fucking *daring* her to get negative now. "I know you will. Vicks will take on some extra shifts. You know she's good for it. She won't let the store sink. You'll see. You'll be just fine." He hugged her tighter.

"Maybe she would," his aunt said glumly, "except she's pregnant. She's going on maternity leave. *Doctor's orders.*" Beverly sniffed and pulled out of his arms, her chin jutting as she smiled in absolute defiance of everything going wrong in her life. When she spoke again, her voice was light, even cheeky. "You know what I think? I think if all these doctors are gonna be giving us all these orders, they should pick up the slack."

She'd cheered up after that, but Christian couldn't bring himself to do the same.

She's losing her whole life to this, he kept thinking over and over. He felt sick. Furious. Helpless. And even though he tried, even though she got out a deck of playing cards to help him try, he just couldn't bring himself to smile for her or be the emotional rock she so obviously needed. He was too weak for this. Too damn weak. At least Sandra was strong. He had to believe that she'd look out for his aunt. Take care of her properly, lend her a little of that fighting spirit.

He refused his auntie's dinner invitation, begging off on account of piles of homework. Which was true, but still a shitty excuse, and he and Sandra both knew it. Beverly just smiled and told him to call her Saturday for lunch, as if her whole world wasn't collapsing around her while Christian just stood by watching it happen.

Before he could get out the door, though, Sandra cornered him in the front hallway. "You need to think about your priorities," she said.

Christian didn't have an answer for her. He *certainly* didn't have any kind of comeback.

Where *were* his priorities? His aunt was sick, her store failing, and he was worrying about lesson plans and having to wear a tie? What the fuck was wrong with him?

He berated himself the whole bus trip home, mind going in circles, gut roiling, eyes burning with an unspeakable urge to cry in public. By the time he made it back, the self-hatred had settled in to the point that he went straight to the fridge and, from there, straight to Max's six-pack of Granville Island IPA.

God, was he seriously going to steal from the guy? Then again, with his frankly fucking ridiculous attempt at being a teetotaller, it wasn't like he had his own booze. And even if he weren't giving up absolutely everything in his life for this teaching school thing, he couldn't afford his own anyway. Because of the tuition. Because of these fucking pointless unnecessary clothes. Because of his aunt's illness. God, was she going to fucking *die*? Was that the unavoidable end of this sad story? And when that happened, what would Christian's teaching certificate mean to him then?

He needed a drink. He needed to numb this somehow, and he wasn't *quite* out of his mind enough to think smoking some weed was a reasonable option. Beer though, beer he could forgive himself for. Nobody at teaching school would even know just so long as he kept it off Facebook.

Starting your teaching career on a lie, eh, Christian?

And what do you call the whole don't-ask-don't-tell thing, then?

Beer. He grabbed the beer.

Max was clearly loaded, after all. He could afford it. Call it a rain cheque for all the drinks Christian had refused the night Max had bought the household pizza and Christian had still been entertaining notions of—what, superiority? Obedience? Idealism?

Or hey, worst come to worst, he could blame it on the condensation, like Max himself had with Rob's water bottle.

Decided, Christian cracked one open and sat down at the kitchen table alone to drown himself in it.

Several bottles in, the man himself appeared. In from another run by the looks of it, sweaty again, a bright green Nike athletic shirt clinging to every inch of his chest.

"Is that my beer?" he asked, surveying the bottles strewn across the table and landing on the one in Christian's hand.

Shit, what was he gonna say if this happened? Oh!

"Condensation," Christian slurred. He waved the bottle in illustration. "Condensation alloverem."

"Uh-huh." Max sat down. "You leave any for me?"

"Maybe. I dunno, I drank . . ." He counted. Kept getting lost after four.

"Six. So, the whole pack." Christian couldn't tell if he was angry or not. Never could read Max at all. It was like the guy kept everyone at a distance, like he was always on the outside looking in. Or up there with God looking down. Yeah, that one. Who the fuck did he think he was?

"You can have'm back if you got some whiskey. You gotta drink 'em out of the toilet though."

"See, this is what happens when you walk around with a big stick up your ass, man. You pull the stick out for even a second and you end up spewing shit all over everything."

Christian gagged.

Max wrinkled his nose, then laughed, the sound putting Christian at ease for what felt like the first time in fucking days. "Yeah, that was pretty much the grossest metaphor I ever made. Sorry."

"You should be." Christian edged over, knocking their shoulders together.

"So should you. You're a fucking mess, man. What's this about? I assume you're not celebrating something."

Celebrating the end of the world. "Jus' drinking away my problems like normal people do."

"Oh, normal people who aren't teachers?" Max cracked a smile, peeling the half-finished bottle out of Christian's hand as he did. He took a swig for himself. "Nah, I'm just giving you a hard time. No more jokes about the meter stick up your ass. Promise. You just tell Uncle Max all about it. You got friends in low places?"

"Huh?"

"You know." Max cleared his throat, threw his arm around Christian's shoulder like they were companionable old drunks, and sang a couple bars of an incredibly off-key version of "Friends in Low Places" before falling into humming, like he'd forgot the rest of the lyrics.

"Never woulda guessed you were a country fan."

"You never asked. But for the record, I'm not. My dad was."

"Oh." Christian realized that Max's arm was still around him. It felt warm. Nice, and—God, he was really fucking lonely, wasn't he? What a mess.

He must have made some kind of noise, because Max gave him a squeeze. "Hey. I know you don't really like me and maybe that's half my fault, but you can talk to me, you know. What's up? Has to be something pretty big to make you pound back a case of somebody else's beer."

"My aunt." *No no no we are not talking about this, I am not telling fucking Max about this. I am not telling Max about my problems.*

"Yeah?"

"She's sick. Cancer. Ovarian. She had the surgery but she's been doing chemotherapy too and . . . it just never seems to get better, you know? I keep thinking that this is it, this is the last treatment, it's almost over, but it never is." He gasped for air. Max's arm didn't leave his shoulders.

He'd never talked about this with anyone. There just wasn't anybody he *could* talk to about it. He didn't want to burden his aunt with his feelings, not when she had so much else. His mother, well, no help there. He'd had a couple friends in his undergrad, but nobody close enough to trust with this, and they'd grown apart since graduation anyway.

"I feel like . . . I feel like I should just quit school, you know? Move in with her. Take care of her properly. Stupid me is afraid that if I leave the program, though, they won't let me back in again, and then I'll never get to be a teacher. Where are my priorities?"

No reply to that. It was as good as an *I told you so*.

"And you know, she has this . . . this *store* and it's her pride and joy, it's her last reason for really living and fighting, and she'd *hate* it if she had to work for anybody else again and now the store is failing because she's so sick and she can't work and her manager is going on maternity leave and—"

"Why don't you work for her?"

"What?"

Max pulled his arm away, leaving Christian in a strange, lonely lurch. He tapped Christian lightly on the cheek with just the tips of his fingers, urging him to turn his face until they were eye-to-eye. "Why don't you work for her?" he repeated, enunciating every word. "You know, do a few shifts to help her pick up the slack until she can hire somebody. You seem pretty smart and competent. Like . . . what kind of store does she run, anyway? You wouldn't need some kinda special qualifications, would you?"

"I . . ."

"I know you have more school work than any normal fucking person, but if the store is going under anyway, it can't be that busy. Bring your homework with you. *Make time*."

"I can't."

"Why not, man? If you really want to help your aunt out rather than sitting here sulking, why don't you?"

"Because . . ." His vision swam. *Because she runs a fucking porn store. A seedy, down in the dumps, twenty-five cent peep show, triple-X, all vibrators half-off porn store.* God, his fucking life. He'd be laughing if he didn't think it would turn into crying. "I just can't."

"Bullshit."

Christian looked down at his hands, managing to mumble, "The program says we're not supposed to have part-time jobs." Which was actually true, but he'd have broken the rules if it was anywhere else. Hell, what with the whole cancer thing he could probably get special permission and not break any rules at all, except for the fact that it was a *fucking porn store.* In a program where he couldn't even swear or drink a fucking beer, how could he explain that?

Moral deviant, a voice that sounded kind of horribly like his mother's chimed in. *Bad influence on children. Pervert. Molester.*

"Wow, man. Just . . . wow." *Now* Max was openly disapproving, all the pity and understanding in his face and body language vanishing in an instant. He pushed his chair back, getting ready to stand, and shook his head. "That is something else. Well, I hope it's worth it."

"You don't understand!" Christian protested, suddenly desperate for that very thing. Since when did he care about Max's opinion of him?

Since always, that was when. Since that very first argument over his new clothes. But what could Christian say? It was humiliating and horrible and if anybody could understand, it would be probably-a-drug-dealer Max, but he just couldn't bring himself to admit it aloud.

Because he couldn't face the thought of Max knowing the whole truth and still telling him to do it anyway.

"You're right. I don't." Max stood.

Christian's hand shot out seemingly of its own volition, catching Max by the wrist. "*Please,* Max!"

"Please what, Christian? You want my approval? You're not going to fucking get it. There's nothing worth what you're giving up right now. I thought you were crazy when it was just the beer and the clothes. Now it's your family, too." *Just the tip of the iceberg,* wasn't that what he'd said the day Christian had come home with the new wardrobe? He was right about everything. He was right and— *God, shut up everyone, everything just shut up.*

He still had Max by the wrist. He'd stand up and face him like a man. He just had to lever himself—he gave Max's arm a yank, and Max reared back, pulling Christian to his feet. Pulling him forward, right into Max's personal space. Pulling him forward until they were face-to-face.

Might as well, Christian thought, absurdly, as he pressed their mouths together.

Perfect clarity, *focus*, hit him like a drug. Yes. This was what he'd needed all along. Release. Freedom. This, just this. Maybe now Max would understand how conflicted he was, how much he was giving up, how much—

Max pulled back, tearing his wrist from Christian's grip. "What the fuck," he snarled, and for one long moment, Christian thought he was about to be a gay panic victim, bloodied on this filthy kitchen floor. But then Max just backed out of his space and said, "Christian, you're drunk. Go to bed."

The next morning when he woke up, fully dressed in his own bed, there was a résumé and cover letter on his desk next to his laptop. The cover letter was a mess, littered with drunken typos, but there was no mistaking who it was meant for.

> *To whom it may conern:*
> *I am appliyng fora part ime position at Rear Entrance Videeo to start asson as possible.*

Shit.

CHAPTER four

ear Entrance Video was one of several seedy adult stores that lined Davie Street. Back before Aunt Beverly bought the place, it had been called something generic like 24/7 Adult, but the handwritten paper sign taped inside the front door that read "Entrance in Rear" had been so ridiculously perfect, considering the neighbourhood, that Beverly had rechristened the entire store.

She'd had such high hopes for this place.

Christian had had a few hopes of his own. He'd been hoping to prove Sandra and Max wrong, but standing here now, he knew they were right. He hadn't even walked in the door yet and already the store was looking sad. Someone had peeled off the "1" in the "Must be 18 or Older" decal on the glass so that it said "8 or Older," and even the cheerful rainbow flag sticker was faded and shredded. Not a good start.

Christian loitered on the sidewalk—passersby dodging around him, a few giving him judgmental stares—knowing that the minute he walked through the door, his decision would be made.

Let's be real. I made up my mind when I printed off that ridiculous excuse for a cover letter.

He had an updated version in his hand now, minus spelling errors. If he was going to do this, he was going to do it properly: apply like a normal guy off the street, as if he weren't the owner's nephew just here as a favour.

Hell, he might not even get hired. He held onto that thought as he pushed through the door.

Overhead, a bell chimed, and then he was right in the thick of it, if by "thick of it" you meant walled in on all sides by vagina. He fought the strong urge to back right out again, but then a woman's voice called, "Hey!"

The woman who'd called to him was sitting behind the sales counter, her chin in her hand and an old computer monitor reflecting its blue light on her pale white skin. Judging by the ruby red lipstick and victory rolls in her black hair, this must be the manager, Vicks. Christian had never met her, given his insistence on having as little to do with his aunt's crazy store as humanly possible (so much for that), but Auntie Beverly had talked about her a lot, describing her as "one of those weird white girls who dresses like it's World War II or she's a cast member in *Grease* or something."

She looked . . . okay. Pale, maybe, with circles under her painted-up eyes, but not like someone who needed *Doctor's orders*. Which was to say, not as bad as his aunt.

And then she stood.

"You are *massive*!" Christian blurted.

She was. Where he could imagine she'd once been amply curvy with a nipped waist and a big ass that even Christian could appreciate, now all of that was overshadowed by her huge, rounded belly. She waddled out from behind the counter, levelling him the kind of glare that withered men's testicles.

"Charming," she deadpanned, and he gulped. "Let me guess: Christian, right?"

"H-how—"

"Well, you didn't stare at my tits or hit on me, so you aren't one of our straight creep customers. Awkward gay kid who's obviously never seen the inside of a place like this, you gotta be the boss lady's nephew."

"Uh . . ." Her eyes were still doing that testicle-shrivelling thing, so he tried to look anywhere else. To his left, a wall of blowjob DVDs, women with their faces covered in spunk or their lips stretched around comically large dicks. To his right, a display of clearance . . . what the hell *were* those things? Maybe better to not look too closely. Which left Vicks's belly. Christian could swear he could see something *moving* in there.

"So what are you doing here, Christian? Oh, and don't think because you're related to Beverly I won't kick your ass out of here if you keep staring at my belly like that."

He snapped his eyes to Vicks's face. She blinked back at him pointedly.

"Looking for a job?" he squeaked, and held up his cover letter as Exhibit A.

"And that's what you lead with? Calling a pregnant woman—who happens to be the hiring manager here—'massive'? Lord help you."

Christian forced himself not to ball up his résumé right then and there. "Yeah. You're right. This is stupid. I'll leave. I don't even know why I came." He turned to leave.

"I didn't say that."

Turned back again. Vicks had her arms crossed, tucked in the narrow valley between her huge breasts and huger belly. "It's obvious you're uncomfortable here, which means to apply for this job . . . you must really love your aunt."

Christian let out his breath in a sigh. "I just want to help her out. But if I'm going to be more hindrance than help—"

"Cool it. C'mere. What's that in your hand, your résumé? Gimme." She waved him over even as she retreated behind the front counter and fell back into her seat.

He set the résumé and cover letter down and slid it toward her. She picked it up and flipped through it without reading it. "So are you some kind of idiot, Christian, or are you just that earnestly honest?"

"Huh?"

"You're the owner's nephew. You think I can turn you away? You think you even need to apply at all? Of course you're hired. Just give me your availability and it's as good as done."

"No," Christian said. Not because he was still holding out hope that he wouldn't get hired—his decision was already made on that front, there was no going back and no chickening out now—but because he really did want to do this right. "She doesn't know I'm here right now, and I don't think she'd be happy if she did. In fact, I'd prefer if she *didn't* know, get me? I just want to help out however I can *if* I can. I'm not here to screw things up even worse, and if I can't do the job right, then I'm not helping anyone. So interview me."

"Okay." Vicks shrugged. "Pretend you're not the boss's nephew? Pretend you're just like any other weird gawky gay boy coming in here for the first time? All right, I could use some practice on my improv skills. Follow me to my office then, Mr. Blake." There was no missing the sarcasm, but for what part?

Vicks took him on a roundabout tour, first trundling up to the front door, flipping the OPEN sign to CLOSED and locking the door, then pulling a crinkled Post-it that said BACK IN 5 from her pocket and slapping it to the glass where the 1 in the backwards 18 should have been.

As for the sarcasm, it was for the "office" part, apparently. Okay, maybe *multiple* parts of Vicks's speech could fit the bill, but definitely the office part.

Because it wasn't an office; it was a secret door behind a wall of fat fetish videos. A secret door that led into what was basically a closet. A closet stacked with opened boxes and dusty VHS cases, amongst which Christian could sort of see a desk and two seriously old-looking rolly chairs. Vicks navigated her way through the debris and took a seat behind the desk, leaving Christian to plop down into the other chair with his back to the door. Underneath him, the chair lurched on a left-leaning diagonal, threatening to tip him out before he righted himself.

Broken lift mechanism? he theorized, because it was better than trying to imagine his aunt holed up in here. No wonder she did the paperwork at her kitchen table.

Vicks steepled her hands, looking every bit the serious boss. "All right, Christian. Standard interview. Tell me a little about yourself."

Seriously? Well, he had asked her for that. "Uh . . . my name's Christian, I guess. I'm twenty-four. I go to SFU for teaching school." *I'm sexually repressed, closeted, and have the hots for my drug dealer roommate who may or may not still beat my ass for making a pass at him last night.*

"And what makes you want to work here?"

Because I can't stand to see my aunt lose one more fucking thing to this disease. "What do people usually say to that?"

Vicks's bland interviewer face cracked a little, a smile showing through. "Depends. A lot of applicants treat this place as a joke, so at this point they'll take out their big brass balls, slap 'em on the table, and outright say to me, 'I get to look at titties all day.'"

Christian wrinkled his nose. "Well, at least that's not a danger with me."

Vicks laughed. "No, I don't suppose it will be, considering when you walked in here you looked like you'd just stumbled on a mass grave. Okay, next question, and this is a serious one. Can you really handle this place, Christian? You look a little uptight. Calling you 'clean-cut' would be a total understatement."

Christian looked down at his neat powder-blue button-down shirt and tie and khakis, all clothes he'd bought a couple of weeks ago. "Well, this is an interview, isn't it? I mean, don't judge a book by its cover, right?"

"True enough. Okay. Well, the next question is usually 'Are you a pothead?' but I guess we'll take it as a 'no' with you?"

"Uh . . . yeah."

"Good, good. Now say 'penis.'"

"*What?*"

"Say 'penis,'" she repeated. "Look, I know you probably think this place is a bit of a joke, but it is a pretty delicate business. If you look at customers weird or they think you're judging them or laughing at them, they won't come back. So you have to be able to talk to them without getting flustered or revealing the fact that you clearly have a stick up your ass. Sorry, probably the wrong choice of words with a gay guy."

Excuse you, if I were still having sex, I would be a top, *thank you very much.*

"Penis," he said. His mouth tried to twitch, from nerves maybe, but he managed to smother the expression (or at least he hoped he did).

"Okay, that was an easy one. Now 'pussy.'"

"P—pussy."

"Not quite so good. How about another boy part then. 'Balls.'"

That was easier. "Balls," he recited back, very proud of himself for keeping a completely neutral tone of voice.

"Tits and clit."

"Tits and clit," Christian managed to repeat back without cracking.

"Hard mode," she said. "Gaping anus. Double penetration."

He gripped the edge of the table so hard he thought he was going to carve gouges in it with his nails, but he said both and didn't laugh.

After that, she had him recite the dirty alphabet from "ass-to-mouth" to "whores" (because there weren't any dirty words starting with x, y, or z, apparently). A whole dictionary of filthy words, many of them the kind of slurs he'd never ever *consider* using, running the gamut from sexist to racist to homophobic and back again. But by the end, he'd mastered his poker face to Vicks's satisfaction.

"Okay, so you have the vocabulary down pat. Now it's time for your practical," she said, cracking a bottle of water and taking a long drink without offering him any. Which was outright torture because he was *parched*. "So say I'm a customer and I call you up asking you to tell me the week's new releases."

"Do people really do that?"

"Yep." She slid a piece of paper to him. It was a typed list of movie titles; an invoice from their distributor, by the looks of things. "Here's this week's order. Read them out to me."

"*Seriously?*"

"You want the job or not?"

Christian cleared his throat. *You're doing this for Aunt Beverly*, he reminded himself . . . *and to prove Max wrong about you.* "Okay, uh . . . Your—seriously?—*Your Mom's a Slut She Takes It in the Butt.*" He gasped for air, like he'd been underwater.

"What volume is that, again? I've already seen up to three."

"Volume . . . volume . . ." He squinted at the invoice. "Seriously? Volume *twenty-six*?"

"Click, I just hung up on you. Try again. Next one on the list. This time, see if you can get through it without saying 'seriously' every second word."

Come on, Christian, at least try. We both know this interview is a complete fucking show trial, but you don't need to rub her face in it. "*His Cheating Wife's Boytoy 2*," he read aloud. Well, that wasn't so bad. Then he looked down to the next title. Read it once, then read it again to make sure he was actually seeing what he thought he was.

Put his head in his folded arms and laughed until he cried a little.

He sat up straight again. Cleared his throat. Took a tissue from Vicks and dabbed at his eyes. "*Queef Queens*," he said, blank-faced, completely serious, the corners of his mouth *vibrating* with the effort of keeping them downturned.

Vicks's serious face cracked into a big grin, and suddenly she was laughing too, pounding her fist on the rickety old desk as big hysterical tears squeezed out the corners of her eyes and smudged her perfect cat-eye eyeliner. "Okay, that one *is* funny," she gasped, and then, "Shit, I think I peed a little."

Which, in a truly bizarre turn of events, only made her laugh harder, until she had to excuse herself and make a teetering and incredibly precarious-looking pregnant-lady run for the bathroom.

He got the job.

He thought he'd feel anxious about what he was doing, the dishonesty of it, the danger of being caught, the possibility he might be kicked out of his program, but as he rode the bus home, he realized he was the happiest he'd been in weeks, maybe even since his aunt's diagnosis before the end of his undergrad.

He felt invincible. Like he was doing *good* in the world, which was a feeling he'd thought only teaching could give him. A feeling teaching school so far *hadn't* given him.

Okay, Christian, no need to get ahead of yourself, here. You're helping your aunt, and that feels good, but wait until you do your first shift before you start considering changing careers.

Christian Blake, BA, certified teacher, smut peddler.

He couldn't wait to see the look on Max's face when he told him.

What? No! Absolutely not! No way you are giving him ammunition, what if he decides to pay you back for that drunken . . . whatever the hell it was? What if he tells your professor what you do on the side? What if you get kicked out of the program? Even if he's not a blackmailing asshole, what if he blabs to your roommates and they blab to their friends who blab to their friends . . .

No I-told-you-so was worth that.

His feeling of invincibility fizzled, along with whatever high he was on. And it *was* a high: completely irresponsible, artificial, wrongheaded, *dangerous* . . .

By the time he got off the bus, he was miserable again, and the walk home, long as it was from the nearest bus stop, *still* wasn't enough time to chill out. The minute he walked through the door, he tore the tie from his throat in disgust and then slammed the door behind him, because it was the closest thing to punching the wall he could get away with.

Max, who was on his way out, raised an eyebrow but didn't say anything.

Good. I dare you to try.

Okay, no he didn't. He was feeling plenty keyed up, but it was aggression better spent jerking it or making trolly YouTube comments on Justin Bieber music videos versus baiting his roommate. His roommate who had the reason, if not necessarily the means, to destroy his life.

Maybe even the means. Vancouver was pretty liberal when it came to gay rights, compared to more rural areas of Canada or other countries, namely his mother's (and his own, he supposed) native Jamaica, but he wasn't sure if that overall climate of clumsy acceptance extended to overprotective elementary school helicopter parents. *Pervert. Sexual deviant. Pedophile. Thanks, Mom.*

He let Max pass.

Stormed upstairs, and was so distracted and angry and scared and furious and lonely and depressed and distracted that he didn't realize he was at the wrong room until he'd opened the door and was staring at Max's unmade bed and guitar case and dirty laundry strewn all over the floor.

And then, in a fit of apparent insanity, instead of closing the door again like he was fucking supposed to, he walked right into Max's room. He wasn't sure of what he was doing, why he was in here— looking for dirt on him, maybe, to ensure his silence? Or just curious about the man, where he worked, how he made his money, who the fuck he even *was*? Well, Max had left his door unlocked, so it served him right, and how fucked-up was it that he was thinking that?

He went to the small desk, looking for bills and a last name, or paycheques. Found neither, but did happen upon a cheesy religious greeting card that had a bible verse on the front and a neatly handwritten "Happy Birthday, Matthew" on the inside, and underneath it "Make this the year you come back to Christ."

Interesting.

A couple of candy wrappers. A few guitar picks. A stack of DVD discs, sans cases. Hollywood tentpole releases, mostly: more than a couple of superhero movies, *Blade Runner*, some anime, and the original *Star Wars* trilogy—seemed cool cat Max was a closet nerd—and then, halfway through the stack, an obscure title Christian recognized.

His Cheating Wife's Boytoy.

He'd seen that today. Well, its sequel, technically. On the list of new releases, just before *Queef Queens.*

Genre: bisexual.

Bisexual.

Christian's mouth went dry.

"Can I help you find something?"

Christian startled, the DVDs flying out of his hands and across the desk like a deck of cards in a game of 52 Pickup.

Max.

Shit.

Bisexual Max.

He scrambled to pick them up again. Put them down. Picked them up. "I, uh, uh, do you have, uh . . ."

Max, leaning against the doorjamb with his wiry arms across his chest, waited patiently.

"Well uh, I just, um. Sorry. I don't even know what I'm doing in here. I guess I was just distracted and I accidentally—your door—but then I saw your DVDs and uh—so hey, do you have . . ."

Don't say His Cheating Wife's Boytoy. *Don't say* His Cheating Wife's Boytoy.

"Spider . . . man . . ." He looked down at the discs scattered across the desk. ". . . Three?"

"*Spider-Man Three?*"

"Yeah. I guess I'm just in the mood for a movie with too many enemies, that spits on the origin stories of its hero." He hoped it sounded as deadpan as Max was looking right now as he stood there, watching Christian flail, and smiling with only one-half of his perfectly formed mouth. "So sue me," Christian finished limply.

"Nah, I got nothing against *Spider-Man Three.* My real question is, if that's what you want, then why are you holding *His Cheating Wife's Boytoy?*"

"What?"

Max didn't say anything, just gestured with a tip of his chin.

Christian looked down at his hand, at the one disc he still held. Bright pink letters. *His Cheating Wife's Boytoy.* His face went hot as if Max had slapped him.

With his dick.

Christian made some kind of half-animal noise of disgust. "Jesus, how should I know? How should I know what kinda perverted movies you have lying around?" He started gathering up the discs again into a stack, slammed down *His Cheating Wife's Boytoy* on top, then on second thought shuffled it somewhere into the middle. "Look, I'm sorry I even came in here. Maybe if you don't want me seeing your porn, maybe you should—you should—put your shit away. This room is a mess! And lock your damn door!"

I've turned into a crazy person. A certifiable crazy person.

Get the fuck out of here before you say anything else, crazy man.

Yes, good idea.

"Maybe I wanted you to see it."

What?

Wait, that hadn't been the voice in Christian's head.

That was Max.

"What?" he said, aloud.

"Maybe I wanted you to see it," Max repeated, voice rich and scratchy as an old record. He pushed off the doorjamb, slinking forward until he and Christian were chest to chest.

"You want me to watch porn with you?" *Yuck. No, thank you. Especially not today of all days.* And yet, there Max was, and God, how could Christian hear him breathing so clearly, like he was listening through a stethoscope? Christian knew he should back away, but he didn't.

"If you're into that kinda thing."

"I'm not."

"So what *are* you into, Christian?" God, up close, Christian could see he had hazel eyes, etched with flecks of copper.

Nothing, he should have said. *Teachers aren't into anything. We reproduce asexually. We feel attraction to nothing but report cards.* "About last night . . ."

"Oh, I see." Max's eyes shuttered and he backed off, body language turning from slutty tomcat to withdrawn teenage boy in an instant. "Let me guess, you were drunk, you had no idea what you were doing, you're straight, yada yada. I get it."

"No." *Stop talking. Stop talking. Teacher. Teacher. Teacher.*

Teacher who works in a fucking porn store now, so fuck it, who cares.

"Well, forget it. What I really wanted to say to you when I followed you up here was, I'm sorry for what I said, okay? It's none of my business what you do with your life. You don't even know me. Why the hell should I tell you what to do, and why the hell should *you* listen? I overstepped."

"But you were right." Christian took a deep breath, squashed the sound of his mother's voice in his head, and stepped forward. He cupped Max's shoulder in the palm of his hand. "I went and got a job at my aunt's store just like you said. I've got to take care of her. She's the only family I have. What's being a teacher mean if I have to sacrifice her?"

"Right," Max said, a little breathless. "Yeah, exactly. Good for you."

Here goes nothing.

"And as to what I'm 'into' . . . I'm into *you*."

Wow, hey. That had been pretty smooth. Could have even made it all the way to *romantic*, if he'd left it at that and just *kissed* the damn guy, but of course he didn't.

"I mean, I'm into lots of guys. Well, not lots of guys, but a few. A normal amount. Well, a normal amount for a . . . a guy like me. Well, a guy like me who doesn't do the club thing. A guy like— I'm gay. Not just when I'm drunk. All the time. Gay. But I do—"

Max kissed him.

CHAPTER five

m ax. *Kissed* him.
   Oh, yeah.

All the tension drained out of Christian's body, better than any massage. Max's kiss was forceful and a little sloppy, his tongue piercing clacking against the back of Christian's teeth. Christian didn't have much brain space left to really criticize his technique, though, because he was already thinking of how that same sloppy, pierced tongue would feel wrapped around his knob.

He growled, digging his hands into Max's shoulders, not sure if he was planning on pushing him to his knees like a whore or gathering him in close like a lover. He settled on breaking off the kiss and holding him at arm's length in a bruising grip, asserting his control over their pace and position even if he didn't know what he wanted to *do* with that control, exactly.

"Huh," Max said, twisting in Christian's grip, testing it maybe. "Didn't peg you for the type to—"

"The type to what?" Christian grinned wolfishly. Today seemed to be *the* day for challenging people's assumptions about him. "The type to make you suck my dick?"

So he *was* going to push Max down onto his knees, after all. He tried a little pressure, just to see, and yeah, they were doing this, because Max got the hint and fell to his knees. "There's that, yeah. But I'm thinking more ..."

"Yeah?" Christian let go of Max's shoulders, reaching for his fly instead. Max watched him, something wicked in his eyes. Rolled his shoulders. Cracked his neck. Grinned.

"You're just such a *square*, Chris."

"Don't call me that," Christian warned, giving him a light porn-y tap on the cheek. "'Chris,' I mean, not a square. Although speaking of that . . . Who's the bigger square, the square, or the square who still uses the word 'square'?"

Max sat back on his heels, fondling the front of Christian's thighs and wetting his lips. Christian wished he had big muscles there to flex, but he didn't, so he settled for thrusting his hips out proudly.

"Repurposed *Star Wars* quote." Max smirked. "Nice. You're definitely making your case for not being a total nerd." And how come even though Max was the one on his knees, it was still like he was looking down on Christian?

Well, Christian didn't have to take any of that lip. He fondled his package with one hand, announcing, "The total nerd whose dick you're about to suck." And to prove he was serious, he slipped a hand into the Y of his briefs and pulled out his hard, heavy cock. He gave it a tug. Poked Max in the chin with it.

"Don't get me wrong," Max continued, expertly avoiding getting that dick anywhere near his mouth, outright *dodging* it, his full lips clamping shut when the head got too close. "It's totally hot, you being such a square. Don't know why, but I see you with that shirt buttoned up all the way and I know I need to fuck you."

"What, you got some kind of Urkel fetish?"

"Don't flatter yourself." Finally, *finally*, and on his *own* terms—yeah, Christian sure as hell didn't miss that part—Max leaned forward, bracing himself on Christian's thigh with one hand while the other wrapped around the base of Christian's dick nice and tight. And then he sucked the head into his mouth. A second or two of hot, delicious suction and then a wet pop and cold air and Max was looking up at him and smiling to himself. He looked like the cover of one of the store's blowjob videos with that dick hanging over his upturned face.

Maybe that would make working there more tolerable, if Christian just superimposed Max's face onto all the covers. Worth a try, anyway. No telling how much work he'd be able to get done considering the distraction, though.

No time to weigh the pros and cons, though, because now Max stretched out his tongue, trying nobly to wrap it around the head of Christian's dick. It looked so bright pink against the dark blood-flushed skin there, so wet and fucking—

Christian's knees went weak.

"It's just—" Max paused to run his mouth up and down the left side of Christian's shaft, the round bead of his piercing finding and following some vein Christian hadn't even realized *existed* but God damn he sure as hell knew all about now. "—I see you dressed like that and all wound tight all the time and I think you must be some kinda repressed *freak*—" The right side, now, and the rough callused hand currently wrapped around the base of Christian's dick moved to cup his balls instead. "—and you *know* I gotta test that theory for myself."

You have no idea how freaky I am . . .

Focus. You're in the middle of a conversation.

"And?" Christian spluttered.

And God, maybe I could even tell *you how freaky, after we're done here.*

Let's not get ahead of ourselves. It's just a fuck. He's still the same untrustworthy underachieving scenester douche bag who'd probably blackmail you to hell and back if he found out your dirty porn store secret. Just now he has your dick in his mouth.

"Nothing conclusive yet," Max said like a scientist, then dove in on Christian's dick again, taking four or five inches in one bob of his head. *So good.*

"Need more—*unfgh*—raw data?"

Max pulled off. "Sorry Chris . . . -tian. I always use protection."

What? Oh. "Raw." Ha-ha.

Well, why *not* gay porn jokes? Porn was a part of Christian's life now, and not just in that secretive ten minutes before he rolled over to go to sleep. Full-time porn.

Embrace the porn.

"You should consider rethinking that," he quipped. "Lotta money to be made doing—"

Max reared back, pushing hard on Christian's thighs as he did so and sending him toppling into the desk. Papers and DVDs slipped and scattered, littering the already clutter-piled floor. Before Christian could regain his balance, Max was on him, standing on his own two feet again and pressed bodily against him. Alternately fumbling with the buttons on Christian's shirt and palming his cock. "Shut up, teacher-man," Max said, and maybe something else, but Christian didn't quite catch it. His hands were so fucking *rough*, the hands of a guy who worked damn hard, which didn't fit Christian's assumptions at-fucking-all but who fucking cared? Maybe you got calluses like that from giving a whole ton of handjobs because, holy shit, Max—Max was fucking *fantastic* at them.

Christian's shirt was hanging open now—not sure when that had happened but, whatever, Christian was totally rolling with the punches by now—and Max's palm was skimming up his heaving belly, up and under one hanging half of the shirt to get at his nipple. Pinching and rolling it. Back to his cock again.

No, he couldn't fucking come like this. He wanted to fuck Max, and he was going to fucking *do it*. Before he lost his nerve.

Before he remembered who he was and what the hell he was getting into.

"Hey," Max purred up at him, stretched his entire body upward until their lips touched—was the guy standing on tippy-toes?—and bent Christian back over the desk. "Plan lessons some other time." He licked into Christian's mouth, a big, sweeping, possessive motion, the kiss of a man who wasn't afraid to get a little messy. "Want your dick in me, and you don't even have my pants off yet."

"Mmf," Christian replied. It was true. He was half undressed with his shirt open and his pants around his knees and he hadn't so much as *touched* Max, other than to put his dick in the guy's mouth.

"You kinda suck at this. You're not a virgin, are you?"

Normally, if a guy even *thought* something remotely uncomplimentary about his sexual prowess, that would be enough to wither Christian's dick and send him packing with his, uh . . . tail between his legs. But with Max, he just bared his teeth and straightened his back and used the four or five inches he had on the guy to bully him back onto the bed. "Is that your idea of pillow talk? How about I get my dick up your ass, then you can tell me how much of a virgin you think I am."

"Challenge accepted." Max pulled out of Christian's arms and slithered backwards on the mattress, never breaking eye contact. He peeled his tight shirt up over his head as he went, his tattoo of the Virgin Mary seeming to brighten the room: all pinks and teals and bloody vivid reds. God, the guy was even hotter with his shirt off. Wiry, cut, not skinny like Christian was. Muscles on his arms that you didn't get just sucking up protein shakes.

The striptease continued as Max undid his belt and slipped it from the loops in his jeans, cracking it like a whip before tossing it to the floor, and then his jeans were next and—

"Who's the nerd now?" Christian cocked an eyebrow at Max's bright red Spider-Man briefs. Square or not, at least *he* didn't buy his undies from the kid's section.

Although Max's dick looked gorgeous in them, rock hard and tucked up to the right side, the teeniest little damp spot showing over the head.

Christian jumped out of his khakis and rushed forward, pushing Max back *hard* onto the bed. At first Max laughed, but when Christian fell on top of him, seeking out that damp spot with his open mouth, it turned to a low gravelly groan.

The heady smell, the perfectly bitter taste . . . Christian groaned too, breathing deep, mouthing more and more until he'd made a couple new damp spots of his own. The whole time Max arched underneath him, body rising and falling like a wave but so perfectly fucking passive, not fighting Christian at all, more like *calling* to him, coaxing him in. His body saying all the humble *pleases* his mouth was too proud to say.

"Condoms," Christian said into Max's groin.

"Yeah," Max sighed back, not answering his implied question, like he hadn't even heard Christian at all.

"Condoms," Christian said, more forcefully, resting his chin on Max's belly while he stroked the flat of his palm up and down Max's trapped shaft.

At last, Max looked down at him, awareness returning to his glazed eyes.

"Oh. Yeah. Them. Uh . . ." He squirmed out from underneath Christian and rolled onto his belly, unselfconsciously yanking a wedgie out from between his ass cheeks. He had hairy, pale thighs, but they were shapely—runner's legs.

Not much ass to speak of, but that was all right. What he had looked just right for sinking into. Christian couldn't wait to yank Max's geeky-hot underwear down just past those scrawny cheeks and fuck his ass with his thighs still pinned together. Nice and tight.

Completely oblivious to Christian's plots, still with his socks on, Max crawled up the bed and fumbled around the edges of his mattress awhile, then over to his end table where he opened a drawer and started tossing its contents to the floor. He was looking more and more panicked and Christian was feeling more and more pessimistic—*come on, Christian, it's not the end of the world, you can still blow each other*—when finally an intact condom showed up hidden amongst the torn empty wrappers. The lube wasn't too long in coming after that, although the bottle was old and mostly empty and kind of sticky looking, and Christian decided that if they were going to make a thing of this, he'd better go and buy him a new bottle. The good stuff. His aunt could use the money anyway.

"Sorry." Max's expression was briefly shy and unguarded. "Don't fuck a lot of guys, to be honest. Actually, I—" He bit his lip, white teeth on pink lips and *God,* Christian wanted to kiss him just then. "I don't really fuck a lot of people *period.* Lately."

That was a surprise. Christian hoped it didn't show on his face.

"Well." He shook his head, trying to break up the strange, frankly off-putting candidness that hung between them like cobwebs. "I just hope you've got enough lube for my monster dick."

He'd meant to keep his delivery totally serious, the way porn stars could somehow deadpan deliver the most ridiculous lines, but at the end there his mouth twitched. Then his eyebrow.

Max laughed first. Then Christian did.

Still laughing, Christian got up into the bed with him, wrapped his arms around him, and pulled him into a tight hug. *Just a fuck,* he warned himself, but shit, he'd told this guy about his aunt, hadn't he? So why couldn't he indulge in a little physical affection since his boundary lines were all so blurry anyway? He'd come on Max's back and spank his ass and that would even the score. That was how it worked, right?

But no matter how Christian justified it to himself, it seemed Max was a little weirded out by the hug too, because he wiggled in Christian's arms, loosening Christian's grip on him, then bit Christian's neck and tweaked his nipples, obviously eager to bring it round to sex again.

Well, two could play that game. Christian pushed him onto his back, head to the foot of the mattress, and straddled his hips. Ran his hands up and down Max's abs and chest, pausing when the touch drew a little shiver. The tattoo. Christian was touching his chest piece, the

Technicolor Virgin Mary in her blue veil, holding a floating crowned heart between her hands.

Christian slowed his touch, tracing his fingertips in featherlight drifting motions over the skin. Max's eyelids fell to half-mast, his nostrils flaring, but he held perfectly still, watching, waiting, absolutely fucking stunningly beautiful just then. The tattoo moved with his deep breaths, the heart in Mary's hands slowly pulsing.

Max smiled, and the moment was over. "Like the ink?"

"Mmm, yeah." Christian turned his hand, letting the flat surface of his nails sweep up from Max's nipple to the upper ridge of Mary's halo. Which drew out another delectable shudder.

"Guess you can't get any of your own, eh?"

"What makes you say that?" Christian kneeled up and took hold of Max's hips, guiding him to turn onto his front. Max didn't need any prompting to arch his back and lift his ass, grinding the clothed curve of it against Christian's aching cock. The cotton felt great on the tight bare skin of his shaft, but he knew what'd be even better.

"Well, the teacher thing," Max said, wiggling his hips somewhat urgently, "and the fact that you're naked and I can pretty much see every inch of you."

Not every inch. Christian pulled down Max's briefs with one hand—just below the curve of his ass, just like he'd planned—and traced the corded muscles of Max's back with the other. The touch to Max's back splayed his fingers wide, revealing the tiny hidden lettering etched blue on the inside of his ring finger. Where his wedding band would be, and at the time, he'd meant it to be just as much of a commitment.

Pride, those tiny letters read, although they were too small and blurry for a person to discern if Christian didn't first reveal what they said. And considering the last couple of months, maybe it was for the best that they were illegible.

"Maybe you should check behind my balls," Christian forced himself to joke back, and then he smiled a genuine smile. It was easy to put his guilt aside and slip back into the uncomplicated present: his balls throbbed, and his cock was pointing down at Max's hole like it was magnetized.

"Buy me dinner first."

"*That's* where you draw the line?" Christian reached forward, spreading Max open and brushing a dry thumb over the dark little pucker of his hole. He picked up the world's saddest economy-sized bottle of lube, flicked it open, and drizzled some down like pouring caramel on a sundae, and God, wasn't that apropos because he was craving this just as bad.

When he used one hand to smear the lube around, Max's hole, obviously just as hungry for this as Christian's dick was, twitched and opened a little.

Christian hooked his thumb inside, relishing the sound of Max's broken moan. No pretence at all. "I can fuck this ass for free, but I gotta buy you a steak to get you to rim me?"

No witty quip from Max, not this time. He just whined and twisted on the bed, his hole trying to suck Christian's thumb deeper.

Okay, *fuck* foreplay. Anticipation and flirting and dirty talk and staring into each other's eyes like boyfriends had *all* overstayed their welcome. Christian needed to be balls-deep in that hole *now*.

He pulled his thumb out and got going with the condom, tearing the package with his teeth and rolling the slippery sheath down his shaft impatiently.

Planted a hand on Max's back again, grabbed hold of the base of his dick to point it in the right direction, and plunged right in.

"Fucking *shit*," Max said through gritted teeth.

"That's right," Christian replied. More porno dialogue, but this time it didn't feel awkward at all. "You like that?"

"God, yeah."

"Good, now have the rest."

"The wh—" Max started, but broke off on a shout when Christian pushed the last couple of inches home. Fully seated, he held still, letting Max adjust. Sweat popped up along the skin of Max's back, damp under his hand. Max's muscles rippled, inside and out. He breathed through his nose, in and out, in and out, while Christian waited. At last, he squeaked, "Oh. The *rest*."

"Nothing smartass to say?"

"N-nope, we're cool."

Which was as good an invitation as any. Christian rolled his hips, tracing a circle inside Max's body. Underneath him, Max hummed and moaned, hips shifting as he tried to guide Christian where he wanted him.

"Keep your thighs closed," Christian told him. "Nice and tight for me. Gonna fuck you now."

"Stop talking." But despite his tone, Max did keep his thighs clamped shut, his ass squeezing down deliciously hard.

So Christian stopped talking and pounded him.

And Max took it all.

It felt amazing to let loose, to drop all the bullshit and just fucking *connect* with somebody this way. Naked, but not just that. *Stripped.* Stripped of everything that set them apart, everything that kept Christian hostage, that kept Max hostage, too—no matter what he told everyone, that religious card said he *wasn't* completely free—all of it gone and maybe not forgotten but so fucking insignificant, just for now.

He fell forward, covering Max's body with his own as he jackhammered his hips. Before he knew he was doing it, one hand slipped forward to catch Max by the jaw and turn his face upward for a kiss. Too much jostling movement going on to kiss deeply like they'd been doing, but there was something to be said for that frantic smashing together of lips and teeth, that deep growl in Christian's chest and answering hum from Max, who jerked himself and lifted his ass and took even *more.*

That was it. Everything Max gave, Christian took. Every last inch. Another fumbling kiss, and Christian was coming, emptying himself into Max's body, finally finding the satisfaction he'd been chasing. He kept going, thrusting right through the waves of pleasure hitting him head-on over and over again and threatening to drag him under, reaching down and covering Max's fast-working hand with his own, their fingers interlacing clumsily as they jerked Max to completion right onto the sheets.

"Sorry," Christian mumbled as they collapsed forward together, his face slapping Max's sweaty upturned cheek. Okay, maybe he wasn't sorry at all. He'd made a mess of the guy's sheets, but it had been *so* worth it. But if nothing else, Christian was a considerate, well-mannered young man, so he said it again. "Sorry, man. Sorry."

Max gasped for breath and let it out in a chuckle. "It's fine. You can just take my laundry next time you go to wash yours."

Christian lifted his suddenly heavy head, surveying the strewn clothes and balled old socks and the sweat-damp gym shirt hanging over the back of Max's computer chair, and imagined lugging all that to his aunt's place. And how would he explain it? Another guy's underwear—correction, another man's *Spider-Man* underwear—was a conversation he didn't want to have, especially not with Sandra lurking around. "How about I just take the sheets, and you stop trying to push your luck?"

"We'll iron out the details later," Max hedged. But no fucking *way* Christian was doing his laundry, especially if he was already on the hook for dinner. "So uh . . . not a virgin at all then."

"Told you."

Max's alarm clock read just after 3 a.m. when Christian looked at it. They were tangled together on the bed, still naked and upside down, much as they'd been when they'd finished fucking. It was uncomfortably comfortable.

Christian hazily remembered getting up and disposing of the condom at some point. At the time he'd considered going to bed in his own room, but still overcome by whatever porno sex-god had possessed him, he'd crawled back into Max's bed instead, spooning behind him, stroking him and kissing the nape of his neck until they'd both gotten worked up all over again, traded hasty, mutual handjobs, and then fallen asleep where they lay.

His stomach growled. After an anxious, half-eaten lunch and a skipped-due-to-sex supper, it was no surprise he was waking up at such a god-awful hour.

Or maybe your internal clock is telling you it's time to get the fuck out of here and back to the real world.

Probably the second one, yes. Maybe *Max* didn't have any commitments or any reason to be well-rested and up early, but Christian had class in six hours and had to be on the bus to get there in five, and then, after all that, he had his first shift at Rear Entrance Video from six to eleven.

Man, the real world *sucked.*

All the more reason to get out of Max's bed right the fuck now and never fall for . . . *this* again.

Yeah, that's just Max all over, he thought bitterly as he slipped out of the bed. *An evil drug-dealing queer guy, calling me away from the righteous path with beer and sex and porn.*

And he had the gall to criticize his *mother*? He was just as fucking bad, and the worst thing was, he recognized that in himself and still knew he couldn't ever go back to Max's bed.

Which was all well and good, except for the part where he couldn't find any of his clothes in the tornado of laundry strewn across Max's floor. Well, it was 3 a.m., at least. He cupped one hand over his groin, picked up his backpack with the other, took a deep, fortifying breath as he quietly opened the door, and streaked down the hall to his own room naked as the day he'd been born.

If he never got his shirt and pants back, it would just be the price he had to pay.

CHAPTER six

C hristian was late for class.

Which apparently gave his professor the perfect excuse to spend the half hour after Christian's arrival discussing the so-called "three-strikes system" that led to being kicked out of the program, while everybody else in class alternately looked smugly in Christian's direction or just sick with nervousness. Either way, Christian felt like crap.

If any student made a habit of being "unprofessional," using up their allotted three strikes, that would be the end of their teaching career. Potential "strikes" included, but weren't limited to, being inappropriately dressed (lame clothes: check), badly spoken (no swearing, no slang: working on it), disrespectful to authority (never a problem), tardy (oops), or just unprepared (sigh).

Naturally, the conversation then segued into a discussion of other expellable offenses. "Inappropriate relationships with students" was understandably the most severe of these (especially for an elementary teacher like Christian), but it headed up a whole list of other more minor and nebulously defined infractions, most of them to do with Facebook. But most worryingly of all for Christian was "Any public activity or behaviour that can be construed as unbecoming of a professional teacher, especially if it results in complaints from parents or guardians."

Christian could just picture it: *Excuse me, Principal, but can I talk to you about little Timmy's student teacher, Mr. Blake? I saw him working in a seedy porn store. And because I'm a complaining parent, nobody's going to ask why I was in said porn store to know; they're just gonna jump straight to the part where they crucify that dirty pervert teacher and ruin his life and dreams on just my word.*

So the whole morning was a paranoia-inducing downer, basically. Even the best students, the ones who'd worn business casual *before* the clothing lecture and who always parroted the party line on pedagogy, the ones with 4.0 GPAs and volunteering experience out their perfect asses, were on edge. Of course Christian was a wreck. *Of course* he was!

By the time class was out at half past four, Christian was completely fucking exhausted: mentally and emotionally and physically too. The kind of tired that was so bad and so overpowering you fell asleep on the SkyTrain, backpack-stealing hobos be damned. Except unlike every other long day at school, he couldn't go home and immediately fall into bed. It was the night of his first shift at Rear Entrance Video. After tonight, he would officially be a porn peddler, saying words like "gaping ass" with a straight face, and doing inventory on dildos, and hoping and praying no parents of potential students came in.

His whole life was in some trickster god's hands. Maybe it always had been.

If it happened to anybody else, he'd be laughing.

Which kind of made him a dick, and no wonder his life sucked so bad, seeing as he deserved it, and all. On the topic of Christian-is-a-dick-with-bad-karma, he shouldn't forget the part where he'd snuck out of bed last night without a word and been relieved not to have to face Max this morning. *Nice, well done. Not a prick move at all. Definitely never ever ever going to bite you in the ass.*

Oh well, if he was going to call down drama onto his head by sleeping with a roommate, he might as well go for broke and make it the kind of one-night stand where one party never called the other one again. Which probably worked better for Grindr hookups than with someone you had to share a roof with, dammit.

God, he was completely fucking screwed. At least he hadn't given Max the porn store ammunition necessary to exact revenge, although he had a feeling that even without the ability to ruin his career, Max probably had a million other ways to make Christian's life hell.

And you fucking deserve it.

What the hell had he been thinking? Hadn't he decided to be celibate? Go back into the closet? Hadn't he decided that if he couldn't be celibate, then he could *at least* not sleep with roommates? And since when had he become the kind of person to sleep with a guy and then slip out after? Even with the guys he didn't intend to ever see again, he still went and got a take-out coffee with them the next morning before he deleted them from his phone and his life forever.

He hadn't started this job yet, and already it was turning him into a person he didn't recognize.

Sorry, which job was that? Max's voice, playing Jiminy Cricket, asked. *The porn store one, or the teaching gig?*

Let's not examine that too deeply.

Christian practically fell off the bus when he got to his stop. A heavy Vancouver rain pounded down on him as he walked up Davie Street, perfectly complementing his abject misery.

By the time he reached Rear Entrance Video, he was absolutely soaked. He pushed through the door, the sound of the bell overhead more foreboding than cheerful.

A different girl sat behind the desk, completely ignoring him in favour of a battered copy of *Fifty Shades of Grey*.

"Hey," Christian said. She finally looked up, but she didn't look happy about it. "I'm Christian. I'm here for my first training shift. Where's Vicks?"

The girl, clearly displeased he wasn't just asking her where the blow-up dolls were and then *going away,* rolled her eyes and laid her book down on the counter beside her. "She called in sick, so I'm working a double. Well, a one-and-a-half, because as soon as you know how to use the register, I'm getting the fuck out of here."

"O . . . kay."

"Don't worry, college boy, I'm *pretty sure* you can handle it." She got up. Cracked her back. She was probably nineteen or twenty at most, a little overweight and dressed to hide it in a huge frayed hoodie. Her blonde hair was fried, with mousey-brown roots. She was wearing Day-Glo Adidas high-tops, laces hanging undone and tongues flopping.

Apparently she wasn't planning on introducing herself, so Christian said, "Sorry, what was your name again?"

"Melissa. Let me get you your key."

Just like that? Well, he was the owner's nephew, he supposed. Still, if this was their usual procedure with new hires, it was a damn miracle the place hadn't been robbed ten times over. And she was already trusting him to run the store on his own?

"Okay," she said, handing him the key and watching impatiently as he forced it onto the ring he carried in his back pocket. "Vicks said she didn't get a chance to give you the store tour when you applied, so I guess I'm covering her ass . . . *again*." They were standing next to a tall rack of videos, so that was where they started. "Barely eighteen shit," she said, and then started walking, leading him on a circuit of the tall metal racks. "Blowjobs. Asian fetish. Fat fetish. Miscellaneous fetish. MILFs. Anal. Gang bangs. High-budget stuff. German shit nobody watches because the chicks are fugly but the distributors keep sending it anyway." She barely lingered at each stop, her face not even registering the obscenity of her surroundings. Christian was kind of shell-shocked by it all—all those disembodied vaginas and asses and tits and dicks—but she seemed completely immune, bored even. She stopped again near the back corner of the shop. "Gay and lesbian and—"

He cut her off before she could say the word "shemale," which was happily emblazoned on a bright purple sign above the rack, like it wasn't a fucking slur. "Is this all there is for this section?"

"Uh, yeah."

One rack of Gay DVDs, all muscular bodies and spread asses, which was serviceable enough but probably only half the size of the creepy Interracial section with its endless selection of BIG BLACK DICKS Vols. 1–46 that made Christian feel like some kind of circus animal or genetic experiment.

One rack of "Lesbian" DVDs, which he'd bet dollars to donuts no self-respecting lesbian would be caught *dead* watching.

"Is there a problem?" Melissa asked after a few seconds dumbly watching Christian scowl.

"Well, no, not exactly, but maybe—you'd think—"

Melissa circled a hand in the air, as if to say *Spit it out, I don't have all day.*

"Well, considering the neighbourhood, you'd think they'd have a better . . . uh . . . LGBT selection."

"You'd think," Melissa snapped, then immediately resumed walking, the flip of her blonde ponytail screaming *Not my fucking problem.*

If it was at all possible, the section labeled "Toys and Novelties" was even worse. Half the hooks on the wall were empty. What items were in stock had packages that were dusty and grimy looking, nothing Christian would want to put inside himself, and he couldn't imagine anybody else wanting to, either. A whole shelf of deflated blow-up dolls stared at him through creepy dead eyes. "NO RETURNS," several red signs said, and Christian couldn't imagine anybody returning any of this stuff because he couldn't imagine anybody buying it in the first place.

There was one last stop on their misery tour: the two twenty-five cent peep show booths tucked into one corner of the store.

Christian didn't want to touch the dusty red velvet curtains that enclosed them, but luckily Melissa didn't suffer from such qualms. She yanked one open, revealing a shower-stall sized space with a slot for coins like an arcade machine, a dusty ten-inch screen built into the back wall, and a three-legged stool.

"Do people actually use these things?" Christian couldn't keep the distaste out of his tone.

"A couple regulars, yeah."

"And do they . . ."

"Jerk it? Probably. I suggest just sticking a mop under the curtain at the end of the day."

Which explained why all the not-floor surfaces looked so filthy. If he had to guess, they were probably sticky to the touch, too, not that he was about to test that theory.

So things were worse here than he ever could have thought. And it wasn't like he'd ever been particularly optimistic about the whole thing.

"Anywayyy. I'll show you the computer and then I'm out of here." Melissa yanked the curtain shut again. End of tour, apparently.

He stood and quietly listened as she explained the rental system, the till, and finally the filing system they used to organize the DVD discs. He even managed to keep his anxiety in check long enough to focus on what she was saying.

Christian had worked retail before, so the sales didn't seem too daunting . . . on the computer at least. He had no idea what he'd do if someone came in looking for a dildo, or needed suggestions on a good blowjob video to blow his wad to, but he supposed that was one of those skills that couldn't really be taught, anyway. The filing system was alphabetical, so that was easy enough. There was a huge stack of

DVDs to be filed, at least thirty or forty, which seemed like quite the backlog considering the fact that he hadn't seen a single customer the entire time he'd been here.

"So I guess that's pretty much it." Melissa pulled her coat on and gathered up her things. "Just make sure when you put the discs back in the filing cabinet, you put their cases back out on the shelf so the customers—*pfft*—know they're available to rent."

"Is there something funny?" Christian asked before he could stop himself. *God. Teacher voice.* It was the exact same way his grade eleven math teacher used to react to people making fun of the chalk handprints on his ass.

"What?" She pulled her hair out from the collar of her coat in a jerky movement, rounding on him.

Two options: laugh it off and change the subject, or engage in confrontation. No real competition between them, though; this was his aunt's life on the line. "Is there something funny to you about the fact that we don't have any customers, Melissa?" *Address them by name.* Another teacher-thing. Classroom Management 101.

She glared at him, but the expression quickly turned to a smirk. "Actually, since you're asking, *Christian*, yeah, there is. I mean, why the fuck do anything here at all, right? Who are we even doing it for? Don't get me wrong, I'm not saying close the place down—because I dunno about you, but I kinda like making ten bucks an hour to get my *Fifty Shades* fix—but really, what's the point?"

Christian's face flushed hot. "The point? The point is, this place is my aunt's—well, you know what, I don't have to justify it to you. The point is, my aunt pays you to run this place, not sit around and watch it burn. So maybe it's slow, but I don't see you helping matters much by sitting on your ass when there's a hundred things you could be doing to make this place better."

"Oh, look who it is! Mr. Nepotism, here to tell me how to do my job. Well, guess what, dude. You may be the boss's nephew or bastard kid or whatever she's calling you, but *I* have seniority here. Vicks is gone, and that makes *me* manager." She stormed out from behind the desk, made it nearly to the door, then returned to the counter, snatched up her book, and stuffed it into her purse. "Unless little whiny titty baby's planning on calling his auntie-wanty and getting me fired, in which case this hellhole is all yours. Think you can do my job? Ha! I'd like to see you try!"

Christian took a deep breath, fuming. He couldn't make this worse. He couldn't. "I don't want your job. I just want *you* to take it a little more seriously. Okay? Please?"

Melissa rolled her eyes with a huff. "Whatever," she snarled, then stormed out the door.

Christian pinched the bridge of his nose. Dropped into the chair behind the desk with a miserable groan. Got to work.

He spent an hour angrily filing DVD discs, then another hour angrily putting everything already in the filing cabinet back into alphabetical order, since someone—cough, Melissa—had obviously been putting them away without really worrying too much about organization. Either that, or she didn't know the alphabet yet. He angrily pulled a copy of *Konnichiwa Slutty Asian Schoolgirls* out of the R section and angrily put it into the Ks where it belonged.

Then he spent an hour patrolling the store shelves, moving cases into their correct genre sections.

No customers. Part of him was relieved because the fewer customers that came in, the less likely it was to blow up in his face when one of them knew him. But another part of him was distressed because this was his aunt's *whole life*, and that part made him feel like shit for being relieved in the first place.

He couldn't order inventory yet, but he put it at the top of his rapidly expanding to-do list, which included "new decal for door" and "talk to Auntie about expanding gay section and moving it to the front of store."

Then he started cleaning. And not the quick cursory dusting and mop under the curtain Melissa clearly thought was the extent of her duties. Oh no. Full-on hands and knees Cinderella cleaning. He scrubbed the floors, dusted the DVD cases and merchandise, and then—pulling his T-shirt up over his nose and mouth—got to work scrubbing every last inch of the twenty-five cent peep show booths.

Even with all the work he did, he still had time to burn before the end of his shift, so he got out his homework. At the front of his binder was the sheet of notes he'd taken during today's "lecture," the itemized list of expellable offenses. He tore it out, crumpled it into a ball, and tossed it into the garbage. Then, a moment later, fished it from the garbage, flattened it again, and set it aside on the desk. Took a deep breath, and got to work on his assignment, which was some kind of bullshit "action plan" for dealing with disobedient students. *Talk to student quietly and discreetly in hallway so they don't feel the need to "save face" and escalate conflict.*

At a half hour before closing, a girl wandered through the door. She was built like a linebacker, not really fat but just *big*, maybe a few inches shorter than Christian, who was a certified beanpole. She was wearing a long flowy skirt and Birkenstocks, and had a tattoo of vines of ivy going up and down both arms. Not exactly the kind of clientele Christian would expect in a place like this.

"Hi!" Christian tried his best to appear friendly and professional and welcoming, all things this store obviously sorely lacked. "Welcome to Rear Entrance Video. How can I help you?"

She groaned, rubbing her forehead. "Oh God, can it, dude. I work here, so turn off the charm, wouldja?"

"Oh. Uh. Sorry." Christian sat back in his chair, feeling way more awkward than the situation probably warranted.

"Man, you're as bad as Melissa said, aren't you? Well, I'm Candace. Try not to fire me, okay?" *They talked about me already? They already hate me?* "She asked me to come in and show you how to close up."

Despite her cold greeting, Candace was a lot more easygoing and patient than Melissa, even making a couple of jokes with him as she showed him how to count out the drawer and the float and close the computer system for the day.

"So, about Melissa . . ." he tried at one point, and she just shook her head.

"I know she's kind of a bitch, but she's *my* bitch, you know? We've been working together here since before your aunt took over." Candace's voice was warm and understanding, but simultaneously let Christian know exactly where he stood. They weren't friends. She didn't have his back. She just tolerated him better than Melissa did, that was all. "She's mad you're walking in here and basically taking over when she feels like she's the one who's paid her dues. Just steer clear of her and maybe she'll warm up to you. Or maybe not."

Not my problem, she didn't say, but it was loud and clear.

Seemed "Not my problem" was the theme of the day, not that Christian could talk, what with how ashamed he was of this place. Maybe he should change the name from Rear Entrance Video to Not My Problem Video. The slogan could be "Fuck off, we don't care about your business, perverts."

Great. Awesome.

Candace led him to the "office" and showed him how to deposit the day's profit—thirty-three dollars in cash, eighty-some in credit and debit receipts—in the safe under the desk. The float she hid in amongst a stack of old VHS cases. Guarded by grainy pictures of seventies bush and eighties butts. Well, it would probably be the last place a thief (or anyone) would look.

She waited while he packed up his stuff, then hit the lights and the alarm system and walked him to the door, where she watched him flip the OPEN sign to CLOSED, CUM AGAIN SOON, and lock the door.

He thought maybe they'd part ways then, but she just stood there, arms crossed, face screwed up like she was trying to solve a magic-eye puzzle. "I don't know what your deal is, Christian. You don't seem all that bad to me, I guess. If it means I don't have to go into that gross booth and clean anymore, I'm glad to have you on board. But don't forget: Melissa's my girl. You fire her, and I'm gone too."

Which would leave Christian on his own. He heard the threat loud and clear.

Christian got home at midnight, thinking he could just sneak in with a minimum of questions asked and collapse into bed. Not that he was going to do anything there but toss and turn all night worrying about his aunt's store and the fact that there hadn't been a single fucking customer all night and Melissa was a lazy bitch and Candace was threatening him and he was going to get expelled one way or another, he just *knew* it.

But as he passed the living room door, he saw that Max was still up, sitting on the couch watching reruns of *Married with Children*. He sat up straighter when he spotted Christian and waved him in.

Christian felt relieved to see him, at first, opened his arms and nearly went right in for a much needed kiss, but then he remembered they couldn't be together and he couldn't tell Max about his job—what if Max blabbed to the wrong person? What if it got out? What if Max was even more of a scumbag than Christian had assumed, and he used the knowledge to blackmail him?—and it was fucking crazy for him to be happy to see the guy when he was just one more way Christian's life was going to shit.

Working at a porn store. Banging a drug dealer. Who was a dude. Yeah, the teaching school crowd would sure love that.

He had half a mind to ignore the wave. Walk right past Max. Go upstairs and lock his bedroom door behind him. But instead he sighed and stopped, firmly telling himself, *Don't be a fucking coward.*

There was no missing Max's slightly disappointed look when Christian dropped his pre-hug arms and fell into Noah's easy chair instead of onto the couch beside him—or on top of him. Only for a second, though. The smile was back right away, and Max just stretched out like a cat, like he'd always done, except now Christian realized he wasn't just relaxing, he was showing off. Asking a silent question with his body, a question Christian seriously wanted to answer in the affirmative.

"Missed you this morning, babe," Max said in his gravelly flirting voice. He turned his head to Christian, smiling lazily and knowingly and catlike, again, and the blue light of the television lit up his bone structure and he was fucking *gorgeous, God damn.*

Christian cleared his throat. Fisted the knees of his khakis. Refused to look Max in the eye, so he talked to Peggy and Al on their couch instead. "Yeah, I had class early, didn't want to wake you up."

Oh, now Max was sensing something was amiss. He sat up straight again, the flirtation going out of his posture. "You were in class this long? Or did you—"

"Don't worry," Christian snapped back, suddenly annoyed at the whole fucking situation and Max for getting him into it this deep, "I didn't have a *date* or anything."

"*What?*" After the initial outburst, Max's voice smoothed out again. "Ohhh, you think I thought . . ."

"I started my new job tonight. Listen, I know what you're thinking, man, and it was great—it was really, *really* great—but I was serious about the fact that I'm really busy with school and the new job and I just . . ."

"Don't have time for it to be a repeat thing?" Max finished. There was no hurt in his voice, but there was definite anger in his eyes. "Or are you just worried about how it'll look, you and me together?"

Well, at least be honest with the guy. "Yeah. Something like that."

"You gonna stay in the closet forever? Or just until you retire from teaching?"

Christian had no answer to that. Which apparently suited Max just fine, because he wasn't finished.

"I told you it wasn't just clothes and weed. I *told* you. Man, I thought when you took the job, I thought maybe you got your head out of your ass. I thought maybe the whole changing-everything-about-yourself thing was just a moment of weakness and you . . . Forget it. It's your life. I don't have any right to ask you to change." He got up. "Well, since we're done here . . . Night, Christian."

It was better this way. Simpler, and Christian desperately needed something simple in his clusterfuck of a life.

Too bad he still felt like shit.

CHAPTER seven

i t became something of a daily routine. Get up at six in the morning, shave, work hair pick through his curls, button up shirt. Put on tie. Take bus to school. Spend eight hours arguing about standardized testing and fretting about what district, grade, or school he was going to be assigned to for his practicum and how likely his second job was to be discovered. Grab cheap burger. Take bus downtown. Arrive at Rear Entrance Video just in time for the evening shift. On a good day, do shift change with Candace. On a bad day, do it with Melissa and spend the entire time grinding his teeth. See between zero and three customers all night. Do homework. Clean. Notice all the ways in which the store needed so much more than just cleaning. Worry. Deposit meagre earnings in night safe. Lock up. Take 11:03 bus home. Avoid Max, who turned every encounter into a confrontation just by rolling his eyes or snorting at everything Christian said. Fall into bed just before midnight. Jerk off.

Repeat.

Candace, though she was friendlier than Melissa, was just as lazy. No matter how much cleaning or work Christian did at night, by the next day he'd be three steps behind again. Somebody's Coke spilled on the keyboard. Muddy tracks all over the store floor. DVDs out of order. Cases not put away. Cash register not balanced. And that was just the day-to-day stuff, never mind all the other repairs and renovations the store desperately needed.

He wasn't even drawing a wage—afraid it would fuck up his student loans somehow, or if it didn't, that it would sink his aunt into bankruptcy even faster. Oh, and did he mention the part that his aunt didn't even know he was working here?

Yeah, that too.

Which was why things basically went to hell one Thursday night a couple weeks later, when she walked right in through the front door and found him sitting behind the desk.

"Christian!" she yelped, dropping a manila folder full of paperwork which promptly scattered to the ends of the Earth.

"Auntie!" Christian yelped back, leaping out of his seat and rushing to her side. "I'll get it! I'll get it!"

They both bent for the papers, but Christian threw himself to his knees first, crawling across the floor to gather them all while his aunt looked on in stunned silence, one hand cupping her cheek, palm covering her mouth.

The last paper retrieved, he tapped them against the floor to straighten them and stood. Handed them to her. "Um, hi. So uh . . . I work here now. You look . . ." *Like shit*. She was drawn, much thinner than when he'd seen her last. Even the silk scarf printed with graphic red and green poppies that she wore wrapped around her head wasn't brightening her up. "Like you should be at home."

She waved a hand dismissively. "Well, Sandra said she'd come by, but it's still my store, dammit!" She was a trooper for trying to mask her frustration and helplessness behind her laugh. Christian's heart went out to her . . . which was probably the exact opposite response she was looking for. "Where's Melissa? I had her scheduled for tonight."

"Yeah, well, uh . . . about that. I'm working her night shifts now."

Now Auntie Beverly was frowning, like she was catching up with what was going on and didn't like it one bit. "And Candace?"

Christian toed a scuff on the floor tiles, suddenly unable to meet her eyes. "They split the day shifts."

"And you didn't tell me all this because . . .?"

Christian took her by the hand and led her to the seat behind the counter. He set her folder of papers in front of her, trying to hide his open binder. Not fast enough, though: her eyes locked on his half-finished homework. If it was even possible, her frown deepened.

"Don't worry, I only do it when I've finished everything else. And when there's no customers."

"You think that's why I worry? Oh Christian, Christian, Christian. *This* is what I worry about. I can't believe you let Sandra get to you."

"She didn't!" *Max did. And then I slept with him. And then I got cold feet and broke it all off. And now I can't say two words to him.* "She didn't. Auntie, it was the right thing to do, so I did it. That's all there is to it. It's not even that inconvenient, honestly. Not to, uh . . . act happy about how dead this place is, but I have plenty of time to get my homework done. And I didn't tell you because I didn't want you to worry about me. I promise I'm still keeping up with my school stuff. I want to do this. I want to be here for you."

"Oh, Christian." His auntie heaved a dramatic sigh. She looped one arm around his waist, tugging him against her and hiding her face in his sweater-vest. "What would I do without you?"

I don't know. That's why I'm here.

He knew she was close to crying, so he extricated himself from her grip, turning to the papers she'd brought. "So now that the cat's out of the bag, let's get to business, okay? Why are you here tonight? What's all this?" He spread the papers out in front of them.

"They're customer files. I don't keep them here usually. Just in case. Confidentiality."

"Oh, right." Looking at the papers now, it was pretty obvious. Names, addresses, contact numbers, customer file number, photocopies of their provincial ID. Credit card info.

"These are those customers I was telling you about, the ones who owe late fees. I was thinking I'd get Melissa to call and try to collect before we bill their credit cards. Give them a chance to square things away, you know?"

Christian used the customer file number of a guy named John Montgomery to look up his account on the computer. He had six discs out, all of them Asian fetish. His late fees were almost four hundred dollars. *Four hundred dollars!* There were at least twenty customer sheets here. If they all owed even half that much . . .

"You can do that? Just bill them?" God, why the fuck hadn't she done it sooner?

"Part of the customer agreement. They all sign it before they can rent. Provide a credit card and everything. Now, whether they read it before they sign or pay attention when we explain it . . ."

"Ah. Yeah." Christian could hardly talk. It wasn't like he'd *ever* read the iTunes terms and conditions he frequently agreed to, after all. "But wow, four hundred dollars! That's like, almost a week's pay for Melissa."

"Well, no, Mr. Teacher. More like a quarter— Oh, but I suppose it is half. What does she do, take the pay for her shifts and yours, and give you your half under the table? To help hide the fact that you're working here? How'd you get her to agree to that?"

What?

Oh God. Christian wasn't drawing a paycheque. But his aunt was still doing payroll, and the store was still open for two shifts a day, and as far as his aunt had known—before tonight's revelation, anyway— the store had two workers: Candace and Melissa. Before Christian had started the job, Melissa had been working doubles to take over the shift Vicks had left when she'd gone on maternity leave. The shift Christian was working now.

The shift his aunt thought Melissa was *still* working.

Christian hadn't realized— Hadn't even *thought*— Had just been so damn *busy*—

He hadn't been saving his aunt money at all. Melissa had been *taking* it.

And she hadn't said a goddamn fucking thing! A payday had gone by, and she'd gotten a huge fucking check, and she hadn't said a goddamn fucking thing.

"Well?" his aunt asked, her voice still calm and sweet.

Christian made himself smile, flashing teeth. His aunt didn't have the strength to deal with this right now, not with everything else on her plate. Christian would handle it. He'd have to handle it. One way or another, do this himself. "Oh, you know, Auntie. I can be a real charmer when I want to be."

She laughed and tilted him a mock-skeptical look. "In that sweater-vest?"

He assured his aunt he could make the calls, gave her a kiss on the cheek, and sent her on her way. He'd call her on the weekend for a lunch date. It was all under control.

Except, of course, it *wasn't*. It was a fucking mess. Even though the thought filled him with existential fucking dread, he was going to have to confront Melissa about this. There was no way he could let her go on ripping his aunt off. He'd turned a blind eye to her laziness and bad attitude because of Candace, but this was a step too far. This was hundreds of dollars.

I can still solve this. I can still save it.

He looked down at the stack of papers in front of him and took a deep breath. If they were going to get customers back in here, he needed money for inventory and minor cosmetic renovations, like getting new decals for the door. Maybe if he had enough money he could put up something nice in the window display, instead of the old headless mannequin wearing a sun-bleached negligee that currently creeped out passersby looking like something out of a porno *Silent Hill*.

He picked up the first file. John Montgomery. Dialled the phone number listed at the top of the sheet.

"Hello?" a woman answered.

"Hi, can I speak to John Montgomery, please?"

"Can I ask who's calling?"

Gulp. Customer confidentiality, wasn't that what his aunt had said? He wondered whether the guy's wife knew about his porn habit.

"Blockbuster Video?" Christian tried, lamely.

"Aren't they out of business? Who is this?" The woman was angry now, her voice polite, but absolutely *vibrating*.

"I'll just call back later. Thank you for your time, ma'am."

"Like hell you'll call back later, you'll call back when I'm not here, is that it?" the woman shouted, just before Christian hung up.

Wife. Christian wrote on a Post-it, then added, *I think she's onto us.* He stuck it to John's file. Would an honest attempt at contact be enough for his aunt to bill the guy? Christian wasn't sure. He started a MAYBE pile.

Gerald Chan, one hundred dollars in arrears, promised to come in Friday when he got paid. *Says he'll come in later*, Christian wrote on another Post-it, stuck it to Gerald's file, and put it on top of John's.

Bill Salmond, eighty dollars in arrears, had disconnected his phone. He went into the TO BILL pile. As did Edward Terrance, who owed one hundred and ninety-two dollars and told Christian to fuck himself, he wasn't paying. *Oh yes, you are*, Christian thought as he wrote down, *Jerk. Says he's not paying. That's what he thinks.* Stuck the Post-it to Edward's file with a furious slap of his hand.

Three more wives-slash-girlfriends-slash-daughters. Two voicemails, and he wasn't sure whether he should leave messages or not, so he didn't. Three more men who apologetically said they'd come in when they had cash, one man who claimed his discs had been stolen out of his car and thus he shouldn't have to pay the late fees, a policy Christian didn't think existed. One woman, who likewise told him to fuck himself. Finally, there was Carl Dempsey, who was genuinely sorry and sure, it was fine to bill him, thanks for calling, mate.

By the end, Christian had given up trying to sort the files, unsure of who should be billed and who shouldn't. He just left his Post-its with the results of his phone calls on each file, put them all together in one stack, and decided he'd deliver them to his aunt on the weekend and she could sort them out from there. Hopefully some money would come of it.

Sorting out Melissa, though, that was Christian's problem, and there was no putting it off.

That night when he stumbled through the front door of the house, he made the usual beeline straight to his room. Don't talk to anyone, in case you end up standing in one place long enough for Max to cross your path. Don't greet anybody, in case you get sucked into a conversation. Don't go to the kitchen for a drink, in case you're not alone in there and you have to greet anybody. Don't stop for any goddamn reason. Do not collect two hundred dollars.

He closed his bedroom door behind him, flopping back against it like a girl in a seventies slasher flick.

And like a seventies slasher flick, just when he thought he was safe, it all went to hell.

Someone knocked on his door.

"Christian?"

Ugh. *Rob* was knocking on his door. There was no ignoring Rob. Christian would just end up looking like a dick.

He spun, took a fortifying deep breath, and opened the door a crack. "Hey . . . man, what's up?" He'd been an inch away from calling Rob "little man," and diminutive pet names for Rob were *Max's* thing, dammit.

"Open up, noob," another voice—more confident than Rob's—said. "What you doing, jackin' it?"

Oh, so Noah was out there too. Dammit. Were they all out there? Was this some kind of intervention? *Christian, we love you and we care about you. We know about the porn store. You need to stop this.*

He opened the door. Thankfully it was just Rob and Noah standing there. No sign of Max. That was the important thing. "What's up, guys? I was just about to go to bed."

"Well, we wouldn't *have* to come by so late if you were ever home," Rob snapped. Noah dropped a hand onto his shoulder.

"I had to work. *Some of us* don't have rich parents," Christian snarled back, even though he knew it was a bullshit low blow and totally unnecessary. Just . . . he was feeling a little confrontational after tonight's revelation. All keyed up with adrenaline to confront Melissa, but more than that, he was fucking angry at *himself.* That whole paycheque thing. Goddamn. What kind of fucking idiot was he, not to realize that, without knowing Christian was on the roster, his aunt would go on paying Melissa her usual wages?

Sure, Christian had a lot on his plate, but maybe if he could stop worrying about fucking/not fucking his slutty drug dealer roommate, he could have puzzled that one out sooner. *Before* Melissa had got paid for Christian's hours.

Idiot, idiot, idiot!

"Are you okay?" Rob asked, gentle and seemingly not put off by Christian's outburst. Maybe he was used to it. It probably wasn't the first time somebody'd drilled him for having parents who paid his tuition. He was in art school, for fuck's sake. Those guys made a whole identity out of the poorer-than-thou thing. Which didn't make it okay for Christian to get in on the action.

"Yeah, I'm fine. Sorry. And sorry for calling you rich. That was uncalled for." Christian pinched the bridge of his nose and took another deep breath. "What can I do for you guys?"

Rob looked to Noah, who made his I'm-not-your-landlord face, but took charge anyway, just like he always did. "Roommate meeting. Tomorrow. I thought I'd make us all supper. Can you make it?"

"School. Work." *Oh, and also, Max is going to be there.*

"When do you get off?" Rob asked. Not optional, then.

"What time is it now?"

Noah checked his watch. "Eleven-thirty."

"Then that time."

"Okay, so scratch supper. I guess I'll make us a midnight snack instead." For a not-landlord, Noah sure did know how to lay down the law.

"Got it," Christian said.

"Good." Noah saluted him, then headed on down the hall, the soles of his ubiquitous flip-flops slapping the undersides of his feet as he went. Not for the first time, Christian wondered whether the guy wore them when he worked in the kitchen, too.

"Um . . ." Rob hadn't moved. He twisted his lips. Brushed a lock of black hair behind his ear.

"What is it?"

"Can I . . . can I come in for a couple minutes?"

Christian sighed. Not like he was going to sleep anytime soon anyway. "Yeah, sure." He stepped back, letting Rob through.

Rob padded into his room, took a curious look around, and sat on the neatly made bed. Christian crossed his arms and didn't sit beside him.

"What's up?" Christian asked when Rob didn't immediately speak.

"Well, I just . . . I was just wondering if you wanted to talk about anything."

No. No, no, God no. No offense, but not with you. Actually, not with anyone.

No way *anybody* was finding out about Max. Or the fact that Christian was gay, but especially not about Max. He could probably get away with being halfway out of the closet, but he *definitely* couldn't get away with a sleazeball possible drug dealer fuck buddy.

So he couldn't talk to Rob about the sex life situation.

Christian shrugged helplessly. "Do I . . . look like I need to talk about something?"

"Um, kinda?" Rob bit his lip, then nodded firmly. "Yes. Yes, you do."

That didn't sound like Rob was planning on letting this drop without a fight.

Well, maybe Christian could talk with him about the Melissa situation. Just so long as certain . . . triple-X details were edited out, it seemed like an okay idea. Maybe Rob would have some good advice, and even if he didn't, maybe talking about it would alleviate some of Christian's guilt and stress. A trouble shared was a trouble halved, right? Wasn't that what his aunt had always said?

At any rate, if Rob got some kind of confession out of Christian, hopefully he'd go away.

Decided, Christian sat down on the end of the bed, a good couple of feet from Rob. He unbuttoned the top three buttons of his shirt and peeled off his suddenly stifling sweater-vest. "I'm stressed about my job." He tossed the balled-up vest over the back of his computer chair. "I guess I should start at the beginning, though. I have this aunt, right? She's like a second mom to me. I mean, a second mom after my first mom . . . whatever." God, he didn't want to talk about this with Rob. Rob, who had two parents who *loved* him. But maybe Rob hadn't tested his parents the way Christian had. "Well, anyway, I guess the point is, she means a lot to me, my aunt. I totally owe her a lot. So anyway, she has this video store—"

"Those things still exist?" Rob crinkled his nose and laughed. "Who do you rent to, old ladies who still use VHS?"

"Something like that," Christian replied. *Or, you know, nothing like that at all.* "Well, she got diagnosed with cancer last year—"

"No!" Rob exclaimed. That was the way it was with cancer. Other than people who'd been through it, people either acted awkward, or *way* too scandalized, as if cancer was some kind of ultra-rare disease that nobody ever got and it was just *impossible* and *ohhh noooo not her, that's just not fair!*

Christian shrugged off the renewed fear and despair Rob's emotional reaction brought up from inside him. "Yeah. She has good times and bad times. Anyway, running the store has just been too much for her. So I took a job there behind her back . . ."

Playing off Rob's VHS-based assumptions, he told the whole sordid story, more or less, or a G-rated version of the same, anyway. Melissa. Candace. The paycheques. The renovations he desperately needed to do to even *begin* to coax customers back in, because he realized now that there was no "just keeping the store afloat," as he'd first assumed. No floating at all. Sink, or swim. And like hell Christian was going to let his aunt drown. "So you know, there's no profit to really draw on, not after the payroll. And then on top of it all, I've got this lazy-ass coworker taking more than her share of the pay like nobody was gonna notice, and I'm stuck between a rock and a hard place because if I fire her or if she quits I don't have anyone to replace her, you know?" *It wasn't fucking fair.* None of it was. Not his aunt's illness, not the fact that he'd had to take on this stupid fucking job, not the fact that he'd been stuck with shitty employees who threatened him and made his life hell, not— Christian swallowed down what may have ended up being a literal scream of frustration, punching his mattress instead. "What the hell do I do?"

"I . . ." Rob had a glazed look, like he wasn't even listening, or if he was, he wasn't fucking following. Seemed his offer of a sympathetic ear was well meaning, but he'd ultimately bitten off more than he could chew. "Gosh, that's just tough, isn't it? Poor you."

Poor you?

Dammit, Christian didn't need pity, he needed a fucking *answer.* He needed *help.* He needed—

"Why don't you make the employee who got overpaid cough up the extra cash and use that to do the renos?"

Max.

Christian's head snapped up, and both he and Rob turned to the door to gawk. Max was leaning in the doorjamb wearing his workout clothes, the white line of his earbuds cutting down his hard chest. He met Christian's eyes briefly, but there was none of his usual righteous indignation or flirtation or whatever. Just . . . calm.

Christian let that feeling wash over him and took a deep breath, giving Max a little nod in thanks before he remembered they were supposed to be acting awkward around each other.

Which seemed to be around the exact time Max remembered the same, because he shrugged and coughed. "Oh, so-rry," he drawled. "Were you two lovebirds having a private conversation? Maybe next time close the door and don't talk so loud that I can hear you down at the train station." He put his earbuds back in and walked away.

"Man, that asshole," Rob said with a shake of his head. "Anyway . . . what he said. I mean, I'm not exactly a people-person so I don't know how much you should trust my opinion on *anything* like this, but . . . what he said."

He patted Christian's shoulder awkwardly, like a fucking teacher after a *good talk*. Got up. Followed Max down the hall.

What he said.

Right.

CHAPTER eight

t he next morning, Christian woke up feeling more optimistic than he had in ages, although the baseline damn-you're-an-ass level of self-hatred hadn't gone away. In general, things were looking up. Okay, so they were still a mess, but he had a plan at least. He'd take it.

He got up in plenty of time to grab a morning coffee and toast a couple of slices of Rob's bread for breakfast, and was right on time for the train out to school.

He was going to take Max's advice. He was going to just straight-up ask Melissa to give him the money she owed him, and then he was going to invest it in the store. What was good for the store was good for Melissa, he'd tell her. He'd say he knew she didn't mean to take the money, and that he wasn't going to get his aunt involved. He'd say he wasn't even mad. She'd give him the money. He'd fix up the storefront. He'd stand out on the street in a damn sandwich board, if he had to, just to get some people in.

He was going to save his aunt's store.

"I know about the money."

Oh God, teacher voice. So much for not accusing Melissa of anything.

Melissa looked up from where she was doing the afternoon count of the till, her eyes narrowing to little mascara-caked slits. "Excuse me?" she asked, a little Regina George in the delivery.

"The money. My aunt paid you for your shifts and mine."

She blinked and smiled, all fake-sweet and *totally* Regina George. Fat Regina George in ugly sneakers. "Oh? I was wondering why my paycheque was so much. I thought maybe I finally got a raise."

You? A raise? Have you fucking seen this store?

There was a box of inventory not four feet away from them, the pink glittery heads of dildos sprouting out of the packing peanuts like mushrooms. Delivery couldn't have come much later than noon and it was nearly six now and the stupid fucking box *still* hadn't been unpacked, despite the fact that the shelves sorely needed stocking. It was hardly going to attract the hundreds of customers they needed to get this place afloat again, but it was a fucking *start*.

"Well, you didn't," Christian snapped. Teacher voice again. He cleared his throat. "I'm not mad, and I'm not accusing you of stealing it or anything, but it *is* my pay."

"I thought you weren't *here* to get paid." She rolled her eyes.

"That's right, I'm working for free. For my aunt. Not for you." He snatched up the calculator they were supposed to be using to count out the till and float. "Look, we'll just do the math right here, you promise to bring me the difference on Monday. I'll use it to fix up the store a bit. You can even give me a couple of suggestions of things you think we should do with it. Like . . . I was thinking of a new mannequin for the window. You can even have the old one if you want."

"What the fuck would I want some old mannequin for?"

"I don't know, you could sell it on Craigslist to some hipster. Or use it in an art project. Set it on fire for some stress relief. Whatever. Look, just get me the money and I won't tell my aunt what"—*you did*, teacher-Christian put in—"happened."

"Damn straight you're not going to tell your aunt." Melissa snatched up the calculator, stabbing at the keys as Christian watched her. Forty dollars in twenties. One ten dollar bill. Twenty bucks in fives. She added them all, then started counting out coins.

"So you'll bring me the money you owe me?"

"Fuck no."

Christian forced himself to stay calm, even though his hands were vibrating. "What?"

"I said no. You're not going to tell your aunt, and I'm not going to give you one fucking penny, and you know why?"

Because you're a heinous bitch sent here to make my life hell, as if it wasn't bad enough already?

"I'll tell you why. Because of *this*." She dropped her handful of quarters uncounted back into the till drawer and opened the box they used for the float. Dug under a loose pile of five dollar bills, and retrieved a folded piece of loose leaf. Held it out in front of him.

"Wha—?"

While he watched, she opened it, one self-satisfied fold at a time. It was *his* handwriting.

A list.

Oh God. A list of expellable offenses.

"Oh yeah. Now you're not so fucking bossy, are you? You think I'm lazy, but you're sitting here doing your dumb teacher homework on shift? You're *just* as bad as me. And oh, hmm, what's this?" She turned the paper around, squinting her eyes as she read aloud, "*Conduct unbecoming of a teacher.* Say, do you think selling porn counts as conduct unbecoming of a teacher, Christian? I mean, I'm thinking, what with you teaching little kids and all, I dunno how well it'll go over if anybody finds out you sell videos of bitches in pigtails and school uniforms sucking dick. Just a thought."

Christian felt like his heart was going to give out, it was beating so hard and fast. "You wouldn't." He only barely reined in the tremble in his voice. He'd lost. He knew it. She knew it.

"You wanna bet? Okay, you tell your aunt about that money, and you see how well it turns out for you." She grinned at him, more baring her teeth than anything. "Anyway, nice talking to you, Chris. I'm gonna knock off early today, go get a slushy. You gonna tell your aunt *that*?"

Christian burned with shame, feeling like his whole body was just . . . going to go up in smoke. Maybe that would be better. Fuck, *anything* had to be better than this.

"No," he said, as dignified as he could manage. He picked up the quarters she'd dropped and started counting them. Right where she'd left off.

When he fell through the front door that night, it was to a light on in the living room and his four roommates shooting the shit.

Right. The roommate meeting. The *mandatory* roommate meeting.

Fuck, just what he needed.

He wove into the living room, giving his forehead an exaggerated rub. "You guys, can I get a rain cheque on this whole . . . thing?" His roommates stared at him from behind a spread of frankly delicious-looking family-style Italian pasta dishes piled into take-out containers from Noah's restaurant. God, Christian was hungry. "I'm not feeling well," Christian finished lamely, but knew there was no fucking way he was getting away with it. And by the look of that food, he wasn't sure he even wanted to.

"Sit," Max said, like Christian was a dog, and Noah looked relieved that he didn't have to say it.

Max. Oh Max, Max, Max.

He could get through this. He'd talk to Max about the latest developments with Melissa after the roommate meeting. Sure, Max still seemed pissed at him about fucking and then flaking, but he'd overlooked that once already to help out with Christian's store problems. Christian had to believe he'd overlook it again. For Christian's aunt, if not for Christian himself. Max would give it to him straight.

In a manner of speaking.

Christian's thundering heart slowed a little, thinking of that. Yeah. Maybe he and Max could get out of here, take a walk down the Drive together. It was a rare clear night, not a drop of rain. It was late, but there was always *something* open. They could take a nice walk, and Christian could buy Max a coffee, and then they could just sit down somewhere and he could tell his whole sad fucking story. Max would help him. Max wouldn't judge him for working at a porn store. What the fuck did Max care about that kind of thing? Maybe he'd be angry at Christian for keeping secrets—not to mention letting those secrets come between them—but that would just mean he'd be honest. Christian desperately needed some honest advice right now.

Rob cleared his throat. "I hereby call this meeting to order," he announced, and by the awkward looks all around, nobody had any idea if he was saying it seriously or just fucking with them.

"Dig in," Noah said, after a second or two of laughs trying to turn into coughs and then back into laughs again. Food: that gave them something easy to focus on. A good distraction. Even Christian could get into that. A big plate of pumpkin ravioli with a walnut cream sauce. A helping of garlic bread.

He made a face when Max took the same but then piled a scoop of penne primavera right on top of his ravioli, as if the two flavours even remotely went together. Their eyes met. Christian tried to smile. Max looked away.

Maybe they weren't going to go on that walk together, after all.

"So what's all this about?" Austin asked through a mouthful of garlic bread. "Not that I don't appreciate the free food, but—"

"I'm moving out," Max said.

"You're *what*?" Christian spluttered, feeling a hunk of ravioli go flying out his mouth and not even caring.

"No!" Austin added. "Why?"

Max looked at Christian briefly, and then turned to face Austin fully. "I'm a wanderer, my brothers. Never stay in one place very long. It's just time for me to move on."

How could he say it like it was no big deal?

Because it isn't *a big deal. You guys aren't dating. This is what you want.*

"And you knew about this?" Austin asked Rob, and he and Noah nodded.

"He wanted to tell you and Christian himself. I was sworn to secrecy! Promise." Rob mimicked swearing on a Bible for emphasis.

He's leaving you alone. No more complications. Simple. Straightforward. No temptation. This is what you want.

But it wasn't what Christian wanted, not at-fucking-all. "You can't."

Everyone turned to look at him. "What?" Rob asked, clearly completely fucking lost.

"Can I talk to you outside, Christian?" Max asked, very politely, and set his plate down.

"Yes. You can." Christian set his plate down, too. They both stood and walked out without another word to anyone else.

When they were out on the porch in the damp evening air, Max shut the door with something that seemed like it was trying really, *really* hard not to be a slam.

He rounded on Christian. "Is there a problem, *Christian*?"

God, Christian had wanted some alone time with him, but not like this.

"I don't want you to go," Christian answered. God, he sounded so desperate. So small. So . . . alone.

So honest.

"That's nice. Why the fuck not?" Max crossed his arms defensively, and in the glow of the porch light, Christian could see he had goose bumps.

"I just . . . I don't. I don't even know why myself. I mean, I'm telling myself this is a good thing and it's what I want but it's fucking *not*."

"What *do* you want, Christian? And I want you to think for a minute before you open your stupid closet-case mouth, because this awkward-as-hell fuck-me-once-then-never-speak-to-me-again thing is driving me fucking crazy, and I am too damn old for that kind of middle school game-playing shit. I'm *not* going to live with someone who half the time looks at me like I'm going to molest him, and the other half like he wants to fuck me senseless. And since I don't have the power to kick you out, I guess it's me who's gotta go."

Christian reached out, cupping Max's chilly biceps and giving it a squeeze. Max shrugged him off.

"Can I tell you something?"

"Is it going to answer my fucking question?"

"Eventually." Max didn't say anything else, or storm back into the house, so Christian assumed he was good to say his piece. "Look, I know it's frustrating, my whole . . . teacher thing. The ties. The shirts. The not drinking. The not . . . being with you. Thing."

"You think?"

"It's just . . . teaching matters. It matters a lot. To me."

"More than being true to what you really are, apparently." And then Max's expression softened. "But less than your aunt."

"R-right," Christian agreed. "It's just, ever since I was a kid . . ."

Ever since I was a kid, I've wanted to teach. I loved sharing knowledge, guiding children to new skills and understandings. I have a lifelong love of learning and I want to share that with others. That was what he'd said in his interview for the program, and the interviewing panel had all smiled and nodded and taken notes.

"No, you know what, that's all bullshit. When I was sixteen, I came out to my mother. She didn't kick me out. She abandoned me. Up and moved back to Jamaica, said if I wanted to be with her and give up . . . my perversion, then I could come too. Jamaica would fix me right up. Canada was too permissive. Anyway, I couldn't do it. I couldn't change who I was—who I *am*—but I was . . . I was scared. Of what would happen if I went there and I couldn't . . . be who she wanted me to be. Toe the line. And I was fucking *angry* with her. You know, because I was gay I was some kind of socially damaged pervert pedophile and I'd never amount to anything, and I was *sick*."

Max hadn't uncrossed his arms, and he didn't speak, but his brow had smoothed. His frown had turned into a horizontal line, giving away nothing, but at least it wasn't angry.

"So, after all that, my Aunt Beverly, she took me in. She helped me get my life on track, tried to heal all the hurt my mom put on me. And she said, you prove her wrong, you be a model damn citizen if that's what you want, *and* you be gay. At the same time. So you know, be a model citizen: I thought, well, I can be a mayor but half of them are perverts anyway. Or I could be a doctor but I'm not smart enough, or I could be a fireman but, well, look at me."

Max laughed, and Christian laughed too, as a reflex. It was watery and weak but it was there, and with Max laughing along, it gave him the heart to continue.

"So I figured, I'm a nerd, I could be a teacher. So I went to college and did an undergrad in arts and got good grades and volunteered and did all of it, and when I applied for teaching school, I *got in*. The interviewers loved me. The professors loved me. The kids I volunteered with loved me. I wasn't some socially stunted pervert, I was . . ."

Now Max was reaching out to him, arms unwinding from his body, hands catching Christian's, weaving their fingers together.

"I felt normal. I felt . . . well, I felt like a superhero. And I guess I just got caught up in my own hype. I did all this so I didn't have to go back in the closet to be a good person, and I wound up putting myself back in the closet anyway."

They came together at last, chests touching, Max's chilly hands cupping either side of Christian's face. "I feel you on the disapproving parent thing. More than you realize. I still don't think you should hide that you're gay, but you were right to want to stay away from me, Christian," he said, staring hard into Christian's eyes. "I'm bad news. You need to keep your nose clean and I'm the last—"

"I don't care." Christian kissed him. "I don't care." Kissed him again. "I don't care."

Because he didn't. He worked at a fucking porn store shilling blowjob compilations and blow-up dolls. What was being gay compared to that, even with a drug dealer for a boyfriend?

"Yes, you do," Max countered, but kissed him back, so soft and dry and chaste that their lips stuck when they pulled apart. "I really wish you didn't, but you do, and you're right to."

"You think because you have a tattoo you're real badass," Christian said, covering Max's hands with his own to keep him from drawing away. "Well, you're wrong. You the least of my worries, *bwoy*." It was his aunt's word, his aunt's accent, but it sounded good in his mouth, just then.

Christian kissed Max again, and this time it was all teeth and tongue, and his arms lowered to wrap around Max's body and pull him in close, just keep him sheltered against the cold, the tightness of his grip pleading *Never leave* as they kissed and kissed and kissed, like no other kiss Christian had ever shared with *anybody*.

"Stay," he said at last, or rather, gasped it. Kissing Max was like running a marathon. He needed to lie down. "Be my boyfriend, or be my fuck buddy if that's what you want. Whatever you want. I'll do better. Promise. Just give it another month. A trial run, and if I fuck up again, then you leave. Or hell, I'll volunteer to leave. But for now, stay."

"Boyfriend," Max said with a nod. "I don't think a sheltered kid like you can really handle being a fuck buddy. No offense."

Christian punched him on the shoulder playfully. "None taken."

Without another word, Max took Christian by the hand and led him back into the house.

At the doorway to the living room, Max paused to poke his head in. Didn't let go of Christian's hand. "Sorry, guys," he said. "False alarm. Guess you'll have to save your latest Craigslist masterpiece for some other time, eh, Robby-boy?"

"*What?*" their three roommates said simultaneously, but Max was already leading Christian up the stairs.

Max was lying back in Christian's bed, his arms spread out languidly and his palms smoothing over Christian's neatly tucked duvet. He smiled, every line of his body spelling out invitation, but for now, Christian just stood over him. Watching him. Soaking up all his easy confidence. Max might have reservations about his suitability to be Christian's boyfriend, even though he'd ultimately relented, but there was no doubt in his eyes about *this*: the way two bodies came together and how damn good it felt. Max understood that truth, and he didn't fight it. Christian didn't *want* to fight it anymore.

So he didn't. He sank forward onto the bed on top of Max, not even bothering to take his clothes off. There'd be time for that . . . later. He didn't just want to fuck Max and get it over with, not this time. He wanted to draw it out: comb his hands through Max's hair, kiss his neck, blow on his ear to see if Max liked it or found it annoying. Something had changed between them.

Or maybe it was just *Christian* who'd changed.

Max was still Max, writhing underneath him, smiling and twisting and kissing him back, biting his lower lip, meeting Christian at every juncture, fearlessly, shamelessly. Giving every bit as good as he got.

But Christian didn't just like him as an ideal. He liked him as a *person*. A person who was kind of a shithead when he played video games and stole expensive water from his roommates and had the apparent reading skills of a grade-school kid. And was honest and principled and secretly geeky and—Christian reached down with both hands, pulling his fly open—wore Iron Man underwear without an ounce of shame. Maybe Christian had *always* liked Max the person, but now he finally had the clarity and the priorities to just fucking admit it to himself.

Max grinned, all teeth, and thrust his hips upward until Christian's palm cupped his rigid cock. Fucked into Christian's hand slowly, biting his lip. Grabbed Christian by the shoulders suddenly. *Pushed.*

They rolled together. Max on top now, staring down at Christian, kissing Christian's neck, opening Christian's trousers. Sexy. Irresistible. Christian loved that smile of his, the bright flash of his tongue ring when he licked his teeth, the way all his lean muscles rippled as he stripped off his shirt.

This wasn't reckless desire anymore, something Christian only acted upon because his life was going to shit. This was genuine want. He *wanted* Max. His body, his cock, his smile, his advice, his companionship. All of it.

Once they were both naked and pressed together again, with Christian's mouth on one of Max's nipples and Max's hands on Christian's inner thighs, Christian was struck by how intense it was, how urgent and powerful and deep this wanting went. All his life he was raised to believe—*wanted* to believe—that desire was a superficial thing, something you worked through and, if you were disciplined and moral, ultimately put aside in favour of deeper, more important pursuits.

Even though his aunt had tried her best to teach him differently, what with all her talks about self-love and self-acceptance, obviously something of his mother's worldview had held on, because up to tonight, he'd been treating sex as an unwelcome distraction.

But not just the act of sex. Max, too. Max, the *person*, who was squeezing their cocks together in the palm of one hand under the auspices of comparing girths. He'd been something to be resisted and pushed aside and overcome, instead of someone to be embraced and appreciated.

He wasn't a jerk-off fantasy or a forked-tongued tempter. Sex with him wasn't running away from the real world, it *was* the real world. Max was real, and the way Christian wanted him . . . that was just as real and just as important as school and his aunt and proving his mother wrong about him and everything else that shaped his life.

He let Max situate himself between his legs, let Max's expert hands touch his balls and thighs and taint, exploring every inch of him. And then Max touched his hole, with dry fingers at first, and then ones coated in body-warmed lube. Let Max kiss him and pet him and slide home inside him, and it wasn't a shameful thing, not even on the receiving end. At its worst, it was a little frightening and a little painful, until suddenly it wasn't, until Max stretched him just right and stroked him from the inside and filled every inch of his body with strange new pleasure.

Then it was good and close and comfortable, his legs wrapped around Max's waist, Max's face pressed to his neck, Max talking him through it all at a hundred miles a minute while Christian just revelled in the physicality of the thing, the want and need that was so human and, no, not shameful at all.

He was gay. A gay man who was a teacher, who worked at a porn store because it was the right thing to do, who had a sketchy boyfriend and, yes, had sex. Not out of some sick compulsion. Because he enjoyed it.

And Max was the one he'd chosen to share this new self with.

He didn't touch himself, just let himself really *feel* the bare friction of his cock rubbing against Max's hard abs, in amongst all the million other sensations Max was giving him. He came like that, lost in the absolute joy of his own body, unleashed, and Max wasn't long following, pushing into Christian with a hard, desperate thrust and a completely unselfconscious grunt before collapsing forward, kissing Christian through the sated pulses and rhythms of his body.

And afterward, when they were lying together with Max gathered to Christian's chest—his breath warm and slow on Christian's bared throat, not yet asleep but not far off—Christian reached down, took Max by the chin, and tilted his head upward until their eyes met. Max smiled at him, sated and happy, and Christian smiled back, pressing a kiss between his eyes. "You're a part of my life now," he promised.

Not a dirty secret. Not anymore.

But just for a second, he thought Max looked a little sad.

CHAPTER nine

When his alarm went off at six on Monday morning, he woke up wrapped around Max's body for the third day in a row, surrounded by Max's intoxicating smell. He hit the alarm quickly, before it had a chance to wake Max, then carefully slipped out of Max's arms and out of bed.

Max was still asleep when he came back from his shower and didn't wake when he dressed, even with all the opening and closing of his dresser drawers as he searched for a clean shirt that wouldn't draw his professor's ire. If he was saying good-bye to the everything's-a-mess-anyway life philosophy when it came to Max, then he was going to give it up when it came to school and work, too. He'd fire on all cylinders. Give his all to *every* part of his weird conflicting life, including the sleazy porn store part. Be more than a model citizen; he'd be the person his *aunt* believed he could be.

Dressed in a crisp checked shirt and polished leather shoes, he found a tie and looped it around his neck, tying it into a lazy half-Windsor as he watched Max sleep. He was acting like a complete sap, and he didn't care.

Max had *wild* bedhead, and he looked a little like a boy when he slept, the sarcastic curve of his mouth softened to a swollen little pout and one curled hand pillowing his flushed cheek. Christian shouldn't just leave him like this. After all, they were dating now; this wasn't a moment-of-weakness thing anymore. Their situation was too precarious, especially considering Christian's past behaviour, for him to be able to slip out without a word and not cause a misunderstanding. So he wrote a little note and left it on the pillow:

Late movie tonight? Your choice.

And then, on second thought:

As long as it's not His Cheating Wife's Boytoy.

He signed it with a simple *C*, which he thought was affectionate, but also masculine, not likely to be construed as overly lovey-dovey. Someone like Rob probably ended a note like this with *XOXO*, assuming he ever got laid.

A light kiss on Max's sleeping forehead, and Christian was on his way, ready to face a completely new day.

In class, he took meticulous notes and participated thoughtfully in conversation. He made plans for a weekend study session with the guy who sat beside him in lectures. Spent his lunch hour working on overdue homework assignments. On the way to work, he gave an old lady his seat on the bus, thinking to himself, *Yeah I'm gay and work at a porn store and like sex—even bottoming—and I'm also the kind of guy who gives up his bus seat to little old ladies.*

When he arrived at Rear Entrance Video, even the evidence of Melissa's day spent slacking didn't bring him down. He counted out the till with her, sent her on her way with a smile and a wave, and got to work. DVDs put away. Toys dusted. Inventory taken. Peep show booths mopped and wiped down and polished to a shine. At a little past eight, he looked up from his homework to find a man standing at the counter, looking bashful as he offered up a handful of cash. One of his customers with late fees, actually here to pay up as promised.

"I thought this place would have closed down by now, honestly," the man admitted as Christian processed the transaction. "You know, gone the way of Blockbuster. It always looked like it was on its last legs. You have it looking pretty clean today, though."

"Thanks," Christian said with a smile, feeling genuine pride. "It's tough going, but I'm just tackling my to-do list one task at a time."

After a couple more minutes of small talk, the man rented two DVDs and bought a bottle of lube, and left with a promise that his discs would be back on time. He'd paid just over fifty bucks in late fees. Not much, but it was enough to replace the decals on the door, which was a start.

Later that night, Christian slammed his textbook closed and took off his dress shirt. Stalked around the DVD shelves, taking a mental inventory and sketching out a new map. Dumped all of the crappy Euro-porn and "Miscellaneous Fetish" DVDs currently taking up prime real estate at the front of the store into a box and tore the signs off the shelf. Dragged the box to the back of the store, where he gathered up all the Gay, Lesbian, and Bisexual DVDs and brought that section to its new place of prominence in the front.

When he had the new shelves arranged to his satisfaction, his eyes automatically drifted to the familiar bright pink lettering of *His Cheating Wife's Boytoy*.

After smiling stupidly to himself for a few minutes, he went and found a sheet of round purple stickers that read STAFF PICK, peeled one off, and stuck it on the front of the DVD case, right above the title. Signed the sticker with his name.

There. Now I'm committed. I'm a part of this place.

He found a Jake Bass title in the gay section shortly after that, and slapped a STAFF PICK sticker onto that one, too. And then there was an older title he'd loved in high school, not that you could ever get him to openly admit to it. That case got a sticker too.

He used five stickers in all. Made a new point on his to-do list to ask his aunt if Sandra had any recommendations for lesbian porn that actual lesbians might watch. Left instructions for Melissa and Candace to pick a few favourites of their own.

Shortly before closing, another man with overdue late fees showed up, putting enough money in Christian's hand to buy a new mannequin for the storefront. The guy rented a couple of DVDs, too. All in all, Christian ended the day with just shy of three hundred dollars in the till that hadn't been there when his shift had started. Three hundred dollars that made *him* feel like a million bucks.

That night, he and Max watched *His Cheating Wife's Boytoy*.

Well, the first five or so minutes of it, anyway.

Less than a week later, Christian put up the new decals, smoothing the bright rainbow flag sticker into place with pride. That night, besides the four or so regulars, three new customers walked through his door: a drunken gay couple who drilled him about whether his staff pick really did come "personally recommended," *wink wink nudge nudge*, and upon hearing his solemn promise that it did, rented it; and a man who purchased a fist-shaped dildo and never once smiled. "That guy's gonna do some serious fisting tonight," Christian said to the nearest blow-up doll once he was alone, laughed, and then wished he could share his sparkling wit with Max. If only he could break this one last taboo and admit to working here. He wasn't even sure why it was still a secret; after all, he no longer had any reason to believe Max would rat him out to his professors, especially not when the gay-sex-with-a-drug-dealer thing was plenty of ammunition on its own. Even so, he'd put so much time and effort into keeping this secret, he was hesitant to let it go. Maybe because once he did and the sky didn't fall, he'd feel like a complete and total ass.

Two weeks later, his new mannequin arrived. Except they'd shipped him a buff man (complete with anatomically correct package) instead of the generic sexy lady he'd requested to replace their current headless monstrosity. Melissa was clawing up and down the walls mad about it, but Christian, upon seeing the guy, just laughed and christened him Fabio. "We're on Davie Street, aren't we?" he asked, absolutely refusing to be put out by Melissa's mood, then strolled over to his somewhat anemic lingerie selection and picked Fabio a banana hammock printed with a tuxedo and bowtie, an XL ladies girdle, and a pair of bright red fishnets. Six new customers came in that night, and after he closed up, Christian gave Fabio in his fishnets a salute and looked up a Halloween showing of *Rocky Horror* to take Max to on a date.

A few days after that, Candace surprised him by spray-painting the ragged old female mannequin bright purple, the shiny color giving her a new lease on life. Together, they dressed her in a feather boa and a red teddy to match Fabio's fishnets. There were so many customers that night he barely even *looked* at his homework. Christian thought he'd pull an all-nighter once he got off shift, but when he got home, Max was waiting up for him, so they went straight to Christian's room. Max promised to just sit quietly and practice his guitar while Christian got his essay done, but their good intentions lasted less than an hour before they were in bed together in some kind of elaborate blowjob competition.

The customers kept coming. The shelves filled with new stock that sold and was replenished again. Christian became well-versed in vibrator technology at the same time he learned that the campier he acted, the more comfortable women were buying their Rabbit Pearls from him. Three or four regulars turned into seven or eight. Some he liked. Some were absolute creeps who left the peep show booths sticky. He learned to be as good at managing drunks and shifty-eyed minors as any bartender.

Homework became the sole domain of his weekends off. School filled his days, Rear Entrance Video his evenings, and Max, of course, his nights. The balance didn't quite work, and Christian still hadn't revealed the nature of his job, but he was *happy*. Overextended and stressed, but so, so happy.

CHAPTER ten

October passed in a haze of cold fall rain and constant activity, and before Christian knew it, it was Halloween.

Max hadn't been able to keep his trap shut about the *Rocky Horror* date, so what was supposed to be just the two of them had turned into a group outing. It was a midnight showing, so Christian had closed up the shop early so he'd be home in plenty of time to change. He'd opted to go as Brad (of course!), and had purchased a thrift store lab coat and non-prescription glasses just for the occasion. He hugged himself a little self-consciously as he came down the stairs, then said to himself *Commit to it*, put his shoulders back, and strode into the kitchen like he owned the world.

Noah was sitting at the kitchen table, dressed in a pretty serviceable Eddie costume and pulling a face as Rob painstakingly made him up a forehead gash with what appeared to be red lipstick.

Rob himself had donned Columbia's sequined rainbow shorts and jaunty jacket. He pulled it off pretty damn well, as slightly built as he was, especially with the makeup and slicked-back hair. Christian whistled in admiration and Rob flushed right through his gaudy rouged cheeks. Then coughed and said, "Thank you. I like your Brad."

"Nerd with a hero complex dressed up as a nerd with a hero complex. That's a stretch." Austin walked right past all of them to the fridge, where he grabbed a beer and cracked it open. Took a drink.

"You're not dressed up," Rob accused.

Austin snorted. "What? Seriously? It's a requirement?" He was wearing his usual Saturday night club-wear, the mating colors of jock douches everywhere: a rugby shirt with the collar popped, pre-washed jeans, and bright white tennis shoes.

"It really is," Noah said. "You're gonna stick out like a sore thumb."

"Well, so-rry I don't have a secret closet full of leather assless chaps and fishnets, I guess," Austin replied with a scoff and a blush.

Noah scrunched up his face. "You aren't legally obligated to come, you know. If you're not into it, then you're not into it. You're gonna bring the whole night down."

The tension in the room was starting to get uncomfortable, and Max hadn't even come down from his room yet. He and Christian hadn't told their roommates about the fact that they were . . . well, boyfriends. Or fucking around, even.

"Hell, no, I am not staying home. I know all about *Rocky Horror*. Girls in fishnets, corsets . . ."

"You could literally go to any bar in the city tonight and see women dressed just as slutty."

This was supposed to be Christian and Max's first date, before the other guys had invited themselves along, and Christian wasn't sure if it was *still* going to be a date or if they were going to be pretending to be just friends all night. Which would be awkward as all hell and hard to keep up once the alcohol started flowing, a point that was going to be sooner than Christian had expected, if the Austin situation got any worse. He was already craving a shot of . . . something.

"Okay, okay. We can still save this," Rob said, standing. He took an exaggerated deep breath, circling his arms like a yoga instructor. He took Austin by the hand, like it was no big deal. Of course, it was a big deal to Austin, who shook him off like he had leprosy. Rob just sniffed, tilted his chin, and said, "Come on, Austin. I have an idea. No assless chaps. Promise."

As soon as they were gone, Noah got up, strode to one of the cupboards, and pulled down a bottle of whiskey and two shot glasses. "One for the road, Brad?"

"Fuck it, yeah," Christian said.

The shot went down hot and horrible enough to make him shudder.

"Hey, so . . ." Noah's face was flat and serious. "How's your aunt?"

Dammit, Rob. Well, at least Christian hadn't trusted him with the Max or the porn store secrets. Although at this point he was more keeping those out of habit than anything else.

"Holding out," Christian replied. "Look, I don't really wanna talk about it."

"My grandmother died of cancer." Noah wouldn't meet his eye. "It happened a lot faster than we thought it would. Diagnosis, and then less than a year . . . I wish I'd spent more time with her before she . . . went. But I'd just got this position at a great restaurant downtown and, well, I guess you always think you have more time than you do. I'm sure she forgives me for not putting my life on hold for her, but I don't know that *I* forgive me, you know?"

"Are you trying to tell me something?" It wasn't a real question. Christian knew damn well what Noah was trying to say.

"I'm just saying, when you first moved in you were busy, but you still went and saw her on the weekend that one time. Now I don't think you've seen her at all in what, a month?"

I'm keeping her fucking store afloat, that's why. I'm doing this for her.

That was his justification, at least, but somehow it still felt hollow. What was the point of saving her store if it meant he didn't get to take advantage of every moment she still had?

Except she's not going to die.

She can't die.

"I'm not trying to guilt-trip you, man. I'm not telling you what your priorities should be. I'm just saying to you as a friend, if the way you're doing things isn't working . . . You can ask for help. I've been where you are. I don't have a lot of spare time and I know we're not really friends the way you and Max are friends, but still. Ask me for anything. Ask *any* of us."

Right on cue, Rob and Austin returned.

If this were a feel-good movie, they'd say, "Yeah, ask any of us," or some other helpful announcement, but instead, Noah just laughed out loud, and as shaken as he was, Christian joined him. A big belly laugh that knocked all the fear and anxiety right out of him.

"You look like a Chippendales dancer," Noah said.

"Watch out, ladies, it's Magic Mike!" Christian added, wiping non-existent tears.

Austin was still in the same jeans, but now he was wearing a black blazer instead of the rugby shirt. He was bare-chested underneath except for a bowtie, and a polka-dot party hat sat askew on his head.

"Excuse you," Austin said, crossing his arms. "I'm a sexy Transylvanian."

Noah gasped for breath. "Is that like when chicks dress up as a sexy bumblebee or a sexy Care Bear or whatever?"

"Like the guy in a jeans jacket can talk."

"I think he looks cute!" Rob squeaked, in a pitch perfect imitation of a defensive teenage girl. "Wait, Max still isn't downstairs? It's almost quarter past eleven. We have to leave soon! I thought *I* was holding us up."

"Where'd you get the bowtie?" Noah asked.

Austin gave it a little tug on both sides, as if to straighten it.

"It's mine," Rob said, distracted, and turned to the kitchen door, as if he was intending on marching up the stairs and dragging Max down by the stretched ear.

Noah didn't let up. "Oh, oh, let me guess. It's some kind of *Glee* thing?"

"No way. Doctor Who." *Max.*

"Oh my God, *Max*," Christian blurted.

Max had dyed his hair a frizzy platinum blond. He was almost nude, except for . . . yep, that was a pair of gold lamé booty shorts. And he'd *definitely* oiled himself up. The getup was patently ridiculous, but Christian still had to cross his legs. He was seriously regretting going in his underwear and a lab coat now.

"Rocky!" Rob cried.

"Doctor Scott!" Max recited back.

"Do I want to know where you got the shorts?" Austin asked, obviously relieved he no longer had to be the butt of the jokes.

Max didn't miss a beat. "Would you believe I just had them lying around?" And then he walked up to Christian, looped his arms around Christian's shoulders right in front of everybody, and planted a kiss square on Christian's mouth.

Maybe nobody would care that he worked at a porn store, Christian thought to himself later that night. They were at an all-night diner, still in costume and drunk as hell (except for Christian, of course), crowded into one tiny booth with a table full of eggs, bacon, pancakes, and nachos, all of it share and share alike.

They didn't care that Christian and Max were together. Had *never* cared, technically, since—despite Christian's illusions to the contrary—they'd all pretty much figured it out the night of the roommate meeting. Nobody acted awkward about the way Max's arm was around Christian's shoulder as they ate, or the way Max fed Christian forkfuls of his hash browns.

They had spent the night singing "The Time Warp" and doing pelvic thrusts and screaming like girls when a bunch of ladies-and-also-men in corsets had squirted them with ice cold water from pump-action water guns. They'd laughed as Dr. Frank-N-Furter had taken Janet *and* Brad to bed. They didn't care that Christian was gay. They knew he and Max had showers together sometimes in the middle of the night, and nah, they didn't mind, just so long as they didn't find any unidentified splatters on the shower tiles.

Why would any of them care that Christian worked at a porn store? Why had Christian ever convinced himself that they would? They'd probably think it was cool. They'd probably want him to take advantage of his free rentals for their next movie-and-pizza night, although God knew how they'd settle on a genre to watch, let alone a specific title.

Christian could tell them right now, while they were all drunk and companionable. They'd probably think he was joking, but that was all right. Maybe he could use this to gauge their reactions. Claim ignorance tomorrow if it didn't go well.

Dammit, it *would* go well. He could trust them.

"You guys," he said, but Max interrupted him, slurring, "Somebody gotta len'me ten bucks for this."

Noah stabbed his fork in Max's direction, sending egg yolk flying. "Max, you fucking freeloader."

"It's okay, I think I know what this is." Austin slapped Noah on the back, gesturing between Christian and Max with *his* fork. "Christian bought your ticket tonight, right? And he's gonna pay for your dinner too, right? You're the girl, right?"

Christian wrinkled his nose. "There's no g—"

"You guys, lay off him," Rob pleaded. "Seriously. He's broke all the time but he has a good reason, right, Max?"

What?

"Yeah, I drink all my money," Max joked, but it was obvious he was covering something. He kept giving Rob looks like, *Shut up, idiot.*

"No," Rob insisted. He smoothed his hair back and lifted his chin defiantly. Had his mannerisms always been this feminine and the makeup made them obvious? Or was he just *really* committed to the drag thing? "Max doesn't have a lot of money because he does a lot of volunteering in the Downtown East Side. You know, with addicts and prostitutes and stuff. He works for money as much as he can, but he doesn't have time for a steady job so he can only do occasional day work. The volunteering stuff is more important. So I don't know how you guys feel about it, but *I* happen to think it's pretty honourable. I'm *happy* to pay for his dinner."

Everyone looked a little chastened at that.

Max laughed it off. "Look, I'm not some kind of saint or anything. Honestly, I think it's a compulsion. Some people, they have to wash their hands three times, I have to help three 'unfortunates' a day. You know my parents are missionaries? Well, I think it runs in the family, except I'm not a Bible thumper." He shrugged. "Gotta get the urge out somehow, so it was either this or I go straight off the deep end and wait at street corners to ambush little old ladies and drag them across whether they want my help or not."

Christian wasn't drunk, but just then he felt like puking.

Max was an honest-to-God good guy. Not just the time he put in or the cause he'd chosen, but even the way he talked about it all. The way he'd kept it a secret. A genuinely good person. Not a drug dealer at all.

And Christian? Christian was a judgmental, myopic asshole who was becoming a teacher for the credibility and to prove his mother wrong. It was all about appearances for him. No wonder he'd been so willing to play along with the tie and the closet and all the rest of it.

To think, all this time Christian had been looking down on Max?

CHAPTER eleven

"**a**re you okay?" Max asked as Christian took off his Brad glasses, carefully folded them, and set them on his bedside table. They always slept together in Christian's room—partially because Max's room was filthy, partly because his computer monitor faced the bed and he had a screensaver of a half-naked woman that kind of freaked Christian out—but tonight Max seemed hesitant to cross the threshold. He hugged himself, his small body lost in the folds of Christian's lab coat. "It's just, um . . . you're really quiet. Did you . . . did you not want to tell the guys about us? Because I hate to break it to you, but I think they already—"

"It's not that," Christian said. *I was happy about that. Overjoyed. Ready.*

Was.

"But it is something."

Christian didn't want to fight. He knew he shouldn't. He was tired and that plateload of fat and grease was sitting in his gut like a Molotov cocktail about to go off. And as angry as he was at himself for judging Max, and for keeping stupid secrets and playing stupid middle school games, somehow he was just as mad at Max, like Max had *made* him keep all those secrets.

Well, maybe he had. He'd let Christian think the worst of him, after all. And because he'd done that, Christian had started thinking they were equals: porn store employee and drug dealer, two sleazy guys in a sleazy but affirming sexual relationship, and Christian had felt a little less terrible about himself for a while. *Had.* "Yeah. You know what? It *is* something."

"So what is it?" Max's voice was just as aggressive as Christian felt. Max had drunk a couple of beers tonight, and he was probably tired, too. This really wasn't the time to have this conversation. If Christian were responsible and mature, he'd put this off until tomorrow when they'd had some sleep and the booze was out of their systems.

"You. The whole secret Mother Theresa thing. What the fuck was that about?"

"Mother Theresa? Shit." Max scoffed. "You mean my *job*? My *life*?"

"Yeah. Why the fuck didn't you tell me, huh?" They were yelling, now.

Max ripped off the lab coat, balled it up, and tossed it at Christian. It hit him in the center of the chest and fell to the floor. "Why didn't I tell you? I don't know, I guess because you didn't really seem to care about who I was beyond whether or not I was willing to suck your dick."

"That's not even remotely fucking true, and you know it."

"No? Okay, prove it. Tell me something about myself. About my personality. About who I am as a person, not just what I do to you in bed."

You like nerdy movies. You're a little embarrassed of how much you care about the world. You put up a front like you don't give a shit. You're pretty decent at the guitar but you're not dumb or annoying enough to want to be a "musician." You're kind of an asshole but I kinda need that. "Your real name is Matthew."

"Wh—"

"Yeah. Your real name is Matthew." Max's eyes flashed, something like fear or humiliation crossing his features when he heard the name aloud. Christian wasn't going to apologize for embarrassing him. He'd brought it on himself. "I saw the card from your parents. The one with the Bible verse and that whole 'Come back to Christ' spiel. I figured you had a couple secrets and I didn't want to pry. I figured you'd tell me in your own time. But you didn't have secrets, you just had secrets from *me*. Secrets you could apparently tell Rob, though."

What was that word they used in Psych? Projecting? Yeah, that. Oh well, it was hardly like Christian could take it back now.

"What, now you're jealous of Rob? I'm not *fucking* him, you know. So what, I confide in him. He's a nice kid." He paused, eyes fierce. "Not like you. You know what he said? He said you thought I was a fucking drug dealer."

"Well, I didn't fucking know, did I? It's not like you were doing a lot to convince me otherwise, now were you?" Christian was fucking *shaking*. He balled his hands into fists. This wasn't his fault. This wasn't his fault. He wasn't in the wrong here. He was a good fucking guy. "And I didn't care, you know why? Because I liked you. I thought, I don't care what his job is and I don't care how he dresses or how he reflects on me—"

Max's face contorted into a snarl. "Oh, how fucking generous. You don't care if I mess up your teaching reputation? Wow, I'm *so honoured* you'd deign to be with a scab like me." He turned, then, like he was about to walk out the door, but stopped himself at the last second. His chest puffed out. "I'm just some charity project, so you can prove to yourself that you're still human underneath the fucking tie. Is that it?" A terrible, almost gleefully cruel realization seemed to come across his features then. "Oh no. No no no. I have an even better theory. You just keep me around 'cause then you have someone convenient to look down on, right? Just keeping me around so the next time you throw your cancer-patient aunt in front of the bus, you can say, 'At least I'm not that guy'?"

Before he knew he was doing it, Christian had rushed forward and slammed into Max, pinning him to the back of his door with an arm barred across Max's throat. "Don't fucking talk about my aunt," Christian spat down into Max's red, upturned face. "Don't you fucking *dare*."

Max's eyes widened in fear, but then narrowed again. He swallowed, his Adam's apple bobbing where it was pressed against Christian's forearm. "Why, don't like what I have to say?" Max's fear and anger turned to triumph at that. "You've never liked what I have to say, and you know why? Because you're a fucking poser coward, Christian. *That's* who you are. You're no hero. You're just some queer, half-black loser who can't fucking *stand* that he doesn't fit in with the WASP Yaletown yuppies, but instead of saying *Fuck those people*, you just keep trying, hoping maybe next time they'll let you in. Well, guess what? They're never letting you in. They're never letting *us* in. We're losers, Christian. Rejects and outsiders and losers and you are *just* like me, and there's nothing you can do to change that, and you *hate* me for it." He took a deep breath, nostrils flaring. "You hate me, and you're jealous of me, because you want what I have. You want to say fuck the world and just be happy, walk away from your mother the way I walked away from my parents, and you fucking *can't*, not even when it's your aunt's life at stake."

"Get out." Christian's voice was low, vibrating with the effort it was taking him not to shout. He reached down—Max *flinched*, and God, it made Christian fucking sick to see him flinch—and grabbed the doorknob. Turned it. Max fell backwards into the hallway. "And stay out."

Max didn't say anything after that. The last thing Christian saw before he slammed the door were the tears glittering in his fierce eyes.

For a while, Christian sat on his bedroom floor just inside the door, hugging his knees and taking deep shaky breaths.

What the fuck had he just done?

It went against everything he knew and believed about interpersonal relationships, everything he'd been taught about managing conflict.

Well, dammit, what else was he going to do, the way Max had been talking to him? *Half-black*? Goddamn. And then those barbs about his aunt . . .

His aunt. Noah was right. Other than the occasional poke on Facebook, Christian hadn't seen her or even talked to her in weeks, not since he'd decided to save her store *and* do well in school *and* let himself not-date Max. The urge to talk to her now had nothing to do with what Max had said, or with proving Max wrong. It was the talk with Noah. No, it wasn't even that. It was the fact that this was the first time Christian'd had a few minutes alone *to* talk to her.

He got up and lurched across his bedroom, to where his lab coat was balled up on the floor, right where Max had tossed it. He shook it out, locating the left pocket, and dug down until he found his cell.

It took a couple of minutes to boot up, the piece of crap, but it was a relief to know that it at least still had a charge. He was strangely anxious to get ahold of his aunt, which was kind of ridiculous: he'd waited weeks, what was another couple minutes?

It vibrated when it turned on. Vibrated again. Again. Again. Again, again, again.

Six missed calls. Three text messages. His heart fell out of his chest.

The missed calls were all from his aunt.

He flipped to the texts: all from his aunt as well.

Christian this is Sandra where r u

answer yr phone

come to hospital

"Oh God." Christian didn't bother calling back, just threw on whatever clothes were closest to hand. Friday's khakis. Mismatched socks. One of Max's band T-shirts, a tight-fitting black and neon-pink monstrosity that smelled so much like him that Christian couldn't help inhaling deeply. It almost calmed him, until he remembered Max wasn't going to be comforting him anymore.

He stumbled down the stairs, pausing only briefly to yank his sneakers on. Rob poked his head out of the living room door. "Christian? I heard yelling, are you okay? Where are you going?"

"Out." Christian cursed under his breath. His hands were shaking too hard to tie his laces. When he looked up, he felt his eyes stinging, and Rob was looking at him with plain-faced concern. Hadn't Christian burned enough bridges tonight? "Hospital. Vancouver General. It's my aunt."

"Do you—"

"Not yet. See you." He yanked the front door open and fell out into the night.

He flagged down a cab on Commercial Drive, hoping like hell he had enough cash on him for the fare. He couldn't take transit like this. He couldn't. As it was, even with traffic relatively thin in the city, the trip by cab felt like it was taking ten hours. When they pulled up outside the hospital, he threw a twenty at the driver and jumped out of the car, running for the front doors.

The disinterested woman at the front desk directed him to ICU.

Not dead.

Not dead.

He recited it in his head as he walked the halls and rode the elevator. "She's not dead," he said, aloud, when he rounded a corner and Sandra was there.

He wasn't exactly expecting a comforting hug, but he wasn't expecting a full-on slap across the face, either. "No thanks to you!" Sandra snarled.

"Ma'am!" a passing nurse snapped, "I *will* have you escorted out."

"It's fine," Christian said, cradling his stinging face. "I'm fine. I deserved it."

"Doesn't matter if you deserve it or not. Not on hospital property, am I clear?"

"Crystal." Sandra gave a curt, not-quite-apologetic nod, and grabbed Christian by the shoulders. He'd be lying if he said her grip wasn't painful. When she spoke next, it was with a lowered, studiously calm voice. "Where the hell have you been? I've been calling you all damn night. What's this on your face?" She wiped his cheek, holding out fingers. Gold glitter. Max.

"It's nothing. I went to *Rocky Horror. Please*, Sandra, where's Auntie Beverly?"

"*You went to* Rocky *fucking* Horror?" she whispered back harshly. "While your aunt was—"

"What, in the hospital? Well, I didn't goddamn know she was here, did I?" God, why was she giving him such a fucking hard time? Was there anybody in the goddamn world willing to give him a fucking break and a little bit of pity? *Max would have. Just like that first night, when he came home to you drunk on beer you'd stolen from him, and he just threw his arm around your shoulders and let you talk his ear off. And then you pushed him away for not being the loser you thought he was. That you kind of wanted him to be.* Something inside Christian snapped. "So I'm *sorry*, I guess, for thinking I could take a fucking night off in between school and homework and working at her store and worrying about how sick she is." He gasped for air.

Sandra's brow smoothed somewhat, and she released her claw-like grip from his shoulders, cupping the sides of his face instead. "You're right. Sorry for slapping you, that was uncalled for. You're trying, aren't you?"

"I'm trying," Christian agreed, and that was it, that was the end of his bravery and resolve. The tears burning his eyes streaked down his cheeks, following the lines of her thumbs. She swept them away. "I'm trying so, so hard and I—"

"All right kid, all right. I believe you. Come on, I'll take you to your aunt." She threw an arm around his shoulders, like they were companionable old drunks, and led him down the hall. Explaining, as she went: "She's in isolation. Pneumonia. They won't let me in because

I'm not family. I shouldn't even be here at all; visiting hours ended ages ago. But they said I could stay and wait for you."

"They won't let you in? But you—"

"But what? We're just friends, Christian. They're not going to risk her life for her roommate." There was a hurt in her voice, a bitterness that Christian had never heard before. The way she said that word. *Friends*.

She wanted to be more.

"I'm sorry," Christian said.

"Not as sorry as I am. Look, Bev's been sick for coming up on a week. She didn't want me to call you and get you worried, but I finally convinced her this afternoon to get herself checked out and . . . well, it wasn't good. They admitted her and got her set up in isolation and I—I don't know what you're going to find when you get in there, because they're not telling *me* anything." She narrowed her eyes, looking at something over Christian's left shoulder. The quiet, dignified pain in that expression twisted his guts.

A nurse approached them, coming from down one of the brightly lit halls. "This is her nephew," Sandra said, once the nurse was in earshot. "The one I was telling you about. Christian Blake."

"Beverly's next of kin," the nurse confirmed. "Come with me, then, Christian."

Christian swallowed his fear and squared his shoulders. "Whatever you can say to me, you can say to Sandra."

Sandra took a sharp breath.

The nurse didn't even blink. "All right. *Both* of you come with me, then."

She led them to a quiet side room, closed the door, and motioned for them to sit on a low, uncomfortable-looking couch. It was only once he'd done as directed that Christian realized how tired and shaky he was. His knees felt like jelly. Sandra took his hand, her palm rough and cool against his own.

He wished it was Max's, then he didn't. This was humiliating and shameful enough without him here to see.

The nurse took a seat across from the couch and levelled him a calm, serious look, every inch the professional. "So, Christian. My name is Isabelle, and I'm one of the RNs overseeing your aunt's care. As I'm sure you know, your aunt has been undergoing chemotherapy for her cancer. One of the side effects of chemotherapy is often neutropenia, which is a condition where the body doesn't have enough white blood cells."

Christian nodded numbly. "Yeah, I know. She had to stop working. Stop her chemo."

"That's right. Do you understand why she had to stop working?"

"Because of the customers. Too much of a chance of someone getting her sick."

"Yes. White blood cells are what fight off infection in the body. Without them, you're more likely to get sick, and the illnesses you contract are more severe. Even though we did everything we could to keep your aunt safe, somewhere along the way she caught pneumonia. And I'm sorry, Christian, but right now she's not doing well."

Sandra squeezed his hand. He had a feeling it was meant to be a comfort for her as much as for him. She wasn't speaking. Was barely even breathing.

"Right now, we have her in protective isolation so that she isn't exposed to anything else. We take all sorts of precautions to make the room as clean as possible, and that nobody goes in there who doesn't absolutely need to. It's not one hundred percent sterile, but it's much safer than having her in a normal room."

Christian sat forward, heart pounding. "C-can I see her?"

"Yes, you can still see her." Isabelle didn't smile, even though by all rights it was good news. "But there's more we need to talk about first. I think it's important that you know exactly what you're walking into. That you know what to expect. We have your aunt on some heavy-duty IV antibiotics to try to cure the pneumonia, but I have to stress that this is a very serious infection and she is very ill."

Very ill.

Not dead.

Very ill.

Christian nodded.

"It's not a death sentence, but she has a hard fight ahead of her. We're doing everything we can to try to keep her here with you and get her healthy enough to get back to her life and her treatments. Right now, though, she's not capable of breathing on her own, so we have her on a mechanical ventilator. It's not going to be easy to look at, but she's in a medically induced coma, so she's not in pain. You'll have to wear a mask, but you can still see her, and talk to her, although obviously she can't talk back. Do you have any questions?"

Not dead.

Christian shook his head. "I just want to see her."

No flowers.

He wasn't sure why that was the first thing he noticed, *the most important thing*, but there it was.

He knew why there weren't any, of course. The nurse had walked him through the hand washing procedure and found him a face mask to wear, then handed him a strictly worded "Fact Sheet" that was more a list of don'ts. No children under eleven permitted. No one not up-to-date on vaccinations allowed. No more than two visitors at a time. Anyone with cold or flu-like symptoms, even mild ones, barred from entry. No fresh-cut or dried flowers.

No flowers, no warmth, no life. Just an antiseptic white room without a window, and a body lying unmoving in a too-neat bed, the only sound the measured hissing of the respirator.

Christian had lived with his aunt long enough to know that she slept with one foot stuck out from under the covers. How many times had Christian walked into her room on Sunday morning to be greeted by one foot sticking out of a pile of blankets and wearing daisy-yellow toenail polish?

The memory made his heart hurt.

He tried to will himself to approach the bed, actually look his aunt in the face, but he couldn't move. The truth was, he didn't want that silent, still body to be *her*. Well, it didn't have to be. As long as he didn't look her in the face, it could be anybody. Schrödinger's cancer patient.

He'd turn around and tell the nurse to let Sandra stay in his stead. Tell Sandra to lie and say she and his aunt were partners. Maybe when this was all over, and his aunt survived, they would be.

"I can't do this," he said, his voice perversely loud in the stillness of the room.

Yes, you can. And you're going to.

Strange, the recriminating voice in his head usually sounded like his mother, but tonight it was sounding a lot like Max.

She needs you. You love her. So what are you going to do?

What kind of person are you, anyway?

The kind of person who stays. He swallowed his fear, picked up a chair, and forced himself to walk to the head of his aunt's bed. Put the chair down. Sat.

From the nose down, her face was all tubes and tape, mouth wedged open by a plastic guard. Above the nose, though, he could almost believe she was just sleeping, her closed eyes peaceful. He placed a palm on her bare forehead. Stroked her skin. Pressed a kiss to her temple through the paper of his face mask.

He should talk to her. It would bring a little life to the room. Maybe she'd hear his voice in her dreams, if she dreamed at all.

"Your store's doing pretty well," he began, for lack of a better conversation starter. Talking about all the things he hadn't had a chance to tell her in the last few weeks seemed somewhat depressing, but a lot better than *How's the coma holding up?* "I have this couple who comes in once a week now looking for *personal recommendations.* I'm starting to suspect they just like the thrill of getting me to talk dirty to them, judging by the fact that they always want specifics. You can't just say 'This is a great gang bang,' to them, you have to— Oh God, I can't believe I'm talking about gang bangs with my aunt. No offense, Auntie, I mean, I guess it's the nature of the business, isn't it? Changed my whole worldview. Now I look at people and I keep trying to guess their fetish. My roommate Noah, I'd bet you ten dollars right now he likes that babysitter stuff."

He laughed.

"I think people like me more now that I work at a porn store. I mean, not that I'm brave enough to tell most people, but I feel like there's a little less of a gap between me and other people. Not that I think I'm better than everyone else or anything, but sometimes I feel like I have to be in order to be a teacher, or like people think I am, what with the ties and all, you know? But now I feel like I don't have to try so hard to be so perfect all the time. I think the apple polisher thing wasn't making me a lot of friends, or not real friends, at least. I start thinking, would this person still like me if they knew I worked in a porn store? And then people I never would have talked to before—

um, like maybe drug dealers?—now I say, yeah, well who am I to judge, I work at a porn store."

Her hands rested outside of the tucked blankets, palms down, so he reached out and grasped one, mindful of the IV tubes.

"I bet you never had a problem with that kind of thing, right? You never gave a shit what anyone thought of you. I bet you wish my mom was that brave. You know, she always thought *she* was the principled one for making all these so-called sacrifices and hard choices in order to be righteous, but lately I've been thinking that it's actually *you* who's the principled one."

Just like me and Max.

"I . . . I guess this is the perfect time to practice telling you. I've been seeing this guy, Max. I think you'd like him—he doesn't give a shit about what other people think, either. He's not some asshole rebel without a cause though, he's actually"—*pretty amazing*—"a really decent guy, making his own way, living by his own morality."

And I could stand having mine challenged by his.

"Although to be honest, it's kind of a little late to be telling you about him—besides the fact that you're unresponsive in a coma, I mean—because I think we're broken up now, if we were ever really dating in the first place. We had a fight. I learned he does all this volunteering and it challenged my assumptions about him and I . . . flipped out. I want to say it's because I'm stressed and overworked—no offense—but I think that's a cop-out, isn't it? Mostly I guess I was mad because he made me feel like . . ."

He swallowed, unable to say it at first. Looked at his aunt's sleeping face and took a deep breath. Maybe admitting it to her would be easier than admitting it to himself. Maybe it would make him accountable somehow.

"He made me feel like I was wasting my time, doing what I was doing. Teaching. Wearing ties. Trying to hide the fact that I'm gay. I kind of felt like an idiot, you know? Like this whole time I've been working so hard and giving up *everything*, when I could just be dressing how I want and acting how I want and still be a good person and do good in the world. After all, *he* does. Oh Auntie, he does so much. And he doesn't even need any recognition for any of it. He has nothing to prove. It's just the right thing to do, so he does it." There was a lump in Christian's throat now, and he realized that beyond being angry at Max, mostly he was jealous and really, really proud. "I could have just fucking helped out at your store in the first place without making a big production of it. Instead, I took the path of most resistance. No, you know what, that's a cop-out too. I took the path most like my *mother's*."

You fool boy, go get him then, he wished she'd say, but she didn't say anything at all.

CHAPTER twelve

h e stayed with her all night. Talking sometimes, and other times just dozing in his seat, lulled by the rhythm of the machine helping her breathe. Watched over her in silence when the nurses came in to check her vitals and change her IV bag. Smiled and said "Thank you" as they left again.

In the morning, when the hospital came back to life from its strange nocturnal half-sleep, he kissed his aunt's forehead, promised he'd be back as soon as he could, and left for school.

He should have gone from the hospital to the house to get changed and pick up his crap and *then* to campus, but he was dead tired, time was tight, and frankly, he couldn't even contemplate the thought of having to face his roommates right now. He wasn't ready to see Max after their fight, but he wasn't ready to see Rob and explain the situation with his aunt, either. He just needed some fucking *space*. Too bad he was too damn poor to disappear to Europe for a couple of months.

Also, he was having a hard time caring enough about school to worry about his appearance. He had more important things in his life than ties and button-down shirts, and he was frankly ready to start *treating* them like they were more important.

I am a different man. I am not my mother.

Of course, one sniff of disapproval and raised eyebrow from his professor, and Christian was wishing he could sink right through the floor. He wasn't made an example of this time, at least. No talks of "expellable offenses," no mention of the much-feared "three-strikes rule," or the fact that his smelly ill-fitting T-shirt probably counted against him on that basis. Of course, the public shaming had been a warning. If he was seriously in trouble, his professor would probably wait until they were alone to drop the other shoe . . .

"You're living dangerously," the girl in the desk next to him whispered once the professor's back was turned. She gave his outfit an exaggerated once-over. *She* was wearing a trim brown sweater-vest over a pink satin blouse, her dark hair swept up into an immaculate ponytail. All female student teachers somehow dressed the same, even though they theoretically had way more options for business casual clothes. It was practically a uniform. "Didn't you hear that Mike Fraser got kicked out last week? I heard he was out on an observation, and he accidentally said the 'S' word in front of a couple of ninth graders."

The girl on Christian's other side—wearing brown slacks and a blue V-neck sweater—hissed, "No way. *I* heard it was because he posted something on Facebook insulting government standardized testing."

"I thought it was a *racist* Facebook post?" a male voice coming from behind Christian's right shoulder said.

"Well, he deserved it, then," Pink-blouse said, looking directly at Christian as she did.

More voices chimed in.

"I bet it was something totally innocent, like he was ten minutes late for an observation or something. I bet they're making an example of him."

"Better him than me."

That got a hum of agreement from about six different directions.

God, they were all living in fucking terror. Afraid of the tiniest missteps, constantly looking out for the one thing that would end their dreams forever. They would become a teacher—at any cost—or they were *nobody*.

"You better straighten up, Christian. First you're late, then you miss a couple assignments, you barely participate in class, and now you show up without your binder or even a pen, looking like you just did the walk of shame."

"Oh my God, Jaime, guys don't *do* the walk of shame."

"They do the strut of ultimate victory."

"Ugh."

Christian slapped his palms on his little half-desk. "You know what?" he said as he stood, and pulled Max's too-small T-shirt down to cover his stomach from where it had ridden up an inch or three. "It *is* a walk of shame when you're a closeted gay guy." God, how loudly had he just said that? Class was still in session. Everyone but the professor—who was still nattering away at his whiteboard without a care in the world—was staring at Christian. Oh well. "And on that note? I have *way worse* things to worry about right now than how I'm dressed after I've just spent the night at the *hospital*. So, if you'll excuse me."

Strut of ultimate victory, indeed, he thought as he walked right out.

It was a little after noon, and pissing down rain. He'd killed a couple hours riding the bus nowhere, but he still wasn't ready to go home. As shameful as it was to admit it, he also wasn't ready to see his aunt again, even though visiting hours would be starting soon. Hopefully Sandra would stop by in his stead. Let her have some time alone with his aunt to make her own confessions.

He'd walked out of class, had no money for coffee or a movie, couldn't go home or to the hospital . . . so he decided to go to the store. Maybe he'd look through some stock catalogues and make an inventory order while Melissa or Candace (whoever was scheduled today) worked the front. If it was Melissa, he could camp out in the "office" and hide from her in peace; if it was Candace, maybe some company would do him good.

He rushed down Davie Street, dodging from awning to awning to stay as dry as possible. The rain was making him smell like wet Max, which was increasing today's general confusion a hundred fold. After today, he'd keep a spare shirt at the store. It'd give him something to change into after school, at any rate. Gay dudes seemed to think his preppy look was kind of cute and harmless, but he had a sense the straight ones thought he was silently judging them. (Which he was, depending on what they were renting, but never mind that.)

Two more quick sprints, and he was finally passing Fabio in the window. Funny, the neon OPEN sign above his head wasn't lit. Not good for business, but an honest mistake. Maybe he'd leave a note somewhere unavoidable. He yanked the door open.

Yanked again.

It was . . . *locked*?

No BACK IN FIVE MINUTES sign, either. But then, whoever was working—undoubtedly Melissa, at this point—had forgotten that, too. He dove into his front pocket with fingers shivering from the cold and pulled out his key. Unlocked the door.

Inside, the store was pitch dark. The alarm hadn't even been disarmed; it was blinking and beeping, about to go off. He quickly entered his code and turned the lights on. Everything was as he'd left it the night before. The store was supposed to have opened over an hour ago. Was Melissa sick? Had she tried to call in?

Christian checked his phone, but he'd learned his lesson from last night and it was still on. There were no messages from Melissa or otherwise—read: Max.

Maybe she knew he had class so hadn't bothered trying. Oh well, he'd get a straight answer from her later. For now, it was a lucky thing he'd come in early. He got right to business opening up the store, counting out the float and stocking the till with it, starting up the debit machine, checking the box under the slot for after-hours returns.

Not long after he turned on the OPEN neon sign and took a seat behind the desk, a man hustled in, shaking out an umbrella.

"You're open!" he proclaimed.

Christian found that he didn't have to force himself to smile at customers, like he once had. "Hi! Yeah, sorry about that, the girl working days is sick. I hope you haven't been waiting long."

"Sick? She been sick all week?"

"Huh?" Christian sat up straighter. "Why would you say that?" Dread curdled in his gut. He was getting pretty tired of that feeling.

"Well, because you guys haven't been open during the days the last couple times I've come by. I figured maybe you were cutting down on your hours because you didn't have enough customers or something. But I work nights, so I can't come in then. I'm glad I caught you open, I need to talk to you."

"We haven't been open?"

But Melissa was here. She was here *every* day to do shift changeover. Well, except for the days when Candace was here. Candace had worked Sunday, Monday, and Tuesday.

"You haven't been open. That's what I said."

"Oh. Well. Sorry." Christian shook his head. This wasn't the customer's fault. He could worry about Melissa later. "What days did you come by?" Or not.

"Yesterday was Halloween, right? Thursday? Okay, so Wednesday, Thursday, and now today."

All of Melissa's shifts. And yet she'd been here when Christian had come to change shifts with her.

God. The store had been pristine the last few times he'd come in. *Shit, shit, shit.*

"Anyway," the customer said. "I want to talk to you about this credit card charge I got."

"Oh, uh." Christian booted up his computer. "Name?"

The customer put an elbow on the desk, trying to see around to Christian's monitor. "Gerald Chan," he said, and leaned back when he realized he couldn't see anything from that angle, not without climbing over the desk and into Christian's lap.

Gerald Chan's file popped up. One hundred and twenty dollars owing in late fees. Hadn't he been one of the ones who'd promised to come in and pay up? Well, it wasn't like lying was some unheard-of thing. Christian had still owed Blockbuster twenty or thirty bucks when they'd gone under.

Gerald reached into his pocket, unfolding a credit card statement, where he'd highlighted a hundred-and-twenty-dollar charge from a company called BLAKE VIDEO INC.

"Oh, uh." *God, how fucking awkward.* "Sorry, man, that charge is our automatic billing of late fees. I know you said you'd come in, but I guess you left it too long. Anyway, I can clear your account on the computer here, at least."

"What?" Gerald's face turned a kind of eggplant purple. "Left it too long? I came in the very next Friday. I'm a man of my *word*."

"Says here you didn't—" *Oh, shit.*

"Well, I fucking did. I came in Friday at noon-ish with a hundred bucks cash—which was all I owed, thank you—and the girl behind the counter said we were all squared up."

"The girl behind the counter."

"You know, that blonde girl you have working days?"

Melissa.

Christian took a deep breath, trying to will himself not to throw up or start shaking. "I'm very sorry, sir. You're right. I'll give you a credit card refund right now."

He took the man's card. Swiped it through the machine. Refunded him the hundred and twenty dollars.

Melissa had pocketed the cash. Melissa, who was scheduled (and getting *paid*) for eight-hour days, but only working . . . what, the hour Christian came in? The hour Christian came in and then the hour before that, just in case he was early?

She was robbing his aunt *blind*.

His aunt, who was in the hospital in a coma on the verge of fucking death—the odds were less than fifty-fifty, he'd looked them up—and Melissa was robbing her blind, and Christian, fucking coward that he was, had just sat back and fucking let her do it.

All because she'd threatened to get him expelled from his precious teaching program.

Melissa gave herself a twenty-minute buffer.

Twenty minutes before Christian's shift was due to start, she wandered in, looking at first like a deer caught in headlights, and then like some kind of surly . . . something. An ugly Pokémon. She mumbled some excuse about being sick, which he placidly accepted, even though he wanted to tell her to get the fuck out and never come back, or call the RCMP on her for stealing, or, or, or. Anything but what he ultimately chose to do.

Which was to very nicely tell her she could go home early, and to get well soon.

She hadn't even pretended to be fucking sick. Not even a fake cough. She was *so sure* of the fact that her blackmail scheme would work, she didn't give a shit whether he believed her story or not.

It made his fucking blood boil.

After she'd left, Christian called up Vicks at home for the password to the security footage for the store, making up some story about a guy stealing a bunch of cock rings. Watched the footage for Melissa's last few shifts. Sure enough, just like today, she'd been coming in and opening the store twenty minutes before Christian arrived. They'd count out the till together, and then she'd go home, having worked an hour and a half, tops, of the eight hours Christian's aunt was paying her for.

The computer automatically deleted footage that was older than two weeks, but Christian watched every single day of those two weeks of videos. Candace showed up on time for every shift, then spent her time split between working and playing solitaire. Melissa skipped ninety percent of her scheduled hours, showing up only at the last minute.

He watched the footage (on fast forward, of course) twice more over the remainder of his shift, in between helping customers and cleaning the disgusting peep show booths, which were seemingly always sticky no matter what he did to them or how often.

He hated them. He hated this place. He hated Melissa. He hated cancer. He hated his stupid fucking professor. He hated all the other students in his program for making his cowardice seem normal. He hated Max for making him second-guess himself about teaching school in the first place.

He hated *himself.*

After he'd closed up, he walked the however-many blocks to the hospital.

"Visiting hours are over," the nurse on his aunt's ward said as he passed the station desk, not even looking up from her novel.

"Please," Christian replied, but stopped obediently nonetheless. He stood in the empty white hallway as the world went on around him, completely uncaring. Somewhere, behind a locked door, his aunt slept on, and yet he *needed* to see her. "I'm in school all day and I work all night. We don't even know if she's going to make it. Please, just let me see her. Fifteen minutes. Just enough to say good night. Please."

She heaved a sigh. "All right. Fifteen minutes. I mean it. I heard you were here all night last night, but that was a special circumstance, you understand? And this is a special circumstance too. Don't expect anyone else to let you in outside of visiting hours. If you have to take a couple weeks off work, or find someone to cover your shift, or get a special dispensation from your school or your teacher or your boss or whatever, then do it. But you can't just be dropping in here at all hours." Her stern face softened. "Come on and wash your hands."

A few minutes later, he was standing in his aunt's room, masked and thoroughly washed. The nurse, silhouetted in the doorway, tapped her watch. "Fifteen minutes," she reminded, and then she closed the door behind her and was gone.

"Hi, Auntie Beverly." He walked to her side and pulled up a chair, less hesitant this time. He was already adjusted to the sight of the tubes and the sound of the machines. Her unnatural stillness. "I hope Sandra came to see you today. She's been worried sick about you, you know. I wonder if you know how much you mean to her." He let out a breath through his nose. "You really left me a mess at your store, you know. I'm going to have to fire Melissa. Candace says she'll quit if I do. And when I do, Melissa's going to go to my professor and tell him where I'm working. He'll kick me out for sure. I'm scared, but I don't see any way out. I can't just let her take advantage of you, no matter what it ends up costing me. I should have stopped her before it got this bad."

I should have—

Before—

So many regrets.

Tears welled up in his eyes, and he bent at the waist, pressing his nose to the back of her hand, just below the IV site. "I've screwed everything up, Auntie. Absolutely everything. I don't know what to do without you. I need you. I'm not ready for you to die."

He stayed there, crying, until the nurse came to collect him.

He was too raw and too chickenshit, still, to go home. Luckily, Sandra seemed happy for the company, so he spent the night there, in the apartment she and his aunt shared. Sandra found him a change of shirt and underwear and made him a big mug of tea, then they huddled together on the couch, watching his aunt's favourite movies.

"I'm going to hate myself if she dies," Sandra said when the credits were rolling on the third DVD.

Christian was half asleep, not awake enough to be discreet. He leaned sideways until his head fell onto Sandra's bony shoulder. It was surprisingly comfortable. "Me too."

CHAPTER thirteen

he woke up to grey daylight and the patter of rain on the window. Sandra had gone during the night and left him tucked in under a throw blanket. He sat up. Stretched. Found his way to the bathroom, where he took a piss and brushed his teeth with his finger (after washing his hands, that was). There was a travel mug of hot coffee waiting for him on the table, a wordless well-wish from Sandra.

Today is the day.

The day for what?

Christian wasn't sure, exactly. If he didn't fire Melissa, she'd sink his aunt's store. If he did fire her, then she'd sink *him*.

If his aunt were well enough to speak, he knew what she'd say: screw Rear Entrance Video, she'd had her chance to make it work and messed it up, and it wasn't worth messing up Christian's dreams, too. But she wasn't well enough to speak, so the only voice was Christian's conscience-that-sounded-a-lot-like-Max. And *that* voice was asking him if teaching was really his dream at all, or if his dream was something else, something a little less concrete—maybe even something unattainable—that teaching was just standing in for, like some kind of surrogate dream?

What did Christian *really* want? If it was his mother's approval, he'd never get it, even if he won the damn Nobel Prize for curing cancer *and* solving world hunger. If it was to prove her wrong about him, he already did that every single day. Or maybe he really did want to teach for teaching's sake. God, when had it all gotten so confusing? Did everyone else in his class have these existential crises?

He'd have to take his coffee *somewhere*, though. Carry it with him into whatever future he chose. He could take it to class with him, where he'd study hard and get good grades and do his dues substitute teaching until he got his own class, leaving his aunt to her own fate, whatever that might be.

Or he could take it with him to Rear Entrance Video, confront Melissa, and accept that whatever consequences came from that decision, they'd be in honour of his aunt.

He picked up the mug, letting the fortifying warmth of it seep into his palm.

Time to go.

His aunt wasn't going to die.

His aunt wasn't going to die, and Christian was going to make sure that, when she beat this thing, she had a successful store to come back to.

A little after nine in the morning, he arrived at Rear Entrance Video's front door with his coffee in hand.

He didn't see much of a point in sitting around brooding over his decision, so he spent the morning doing some extra cleaning and inventory. He ordered a pizza for lunch. The Domino's guy wound up renting a DVD; Christian was slightly disappointed that he didn't pick one of the ones with the delivery guy sticking his dick through the center of a pizza.

While he ate, he fired off an email to his professor, explaining his aunt's illness and the fact that he'd be missing some classes. It wouldn't mean dick-squat if Melissa chose to rat Christian out, but on the off-chance she didn't, then at least he had a built-in excuse to miss school while he covered her (and Candace's) shifts. It was a little underhanded to use his aunt's illness this way, but he was doing it for *her* store. If that wasn't a good enough reason to play the cancer card, what would be?

Like clockwork, Melissa showed up twenty minutes before Christian's shift was due to start.

"Hi!" He gave her a cheerful wave as she walked in.

She rolled her eyes. No hello, just a grumbled, "I was sick again." She walked up to the desk, as if to take her usual place at the till, but Christian wheeled his chair over to block her path. She rolled her eyes again.

Christian just smiled. "Uh-huh. And I'm sure you called my aunt to tell her you're missing shifts, right, so she isn't still paying you?"

"Um, yeah, I called her this morning. She said it's fine."

"Wow, she woke up just for your call? You must be her favourite employee!"

Melissa obviously was in no mood to play twenty questions with him, because she just stared at him blankly. "Can I come do the till changeover now, or what?"

"Yeah, you know, it's funny you say you talked to her, what with her being in a coma 'n'all. And about the whole 'sick' thing, you've been sick for quite a while now, eh?"

Her blank expression turned into a snarl. "What about it, huh?"

"You're fired, Melissa. Now. Go. I'll mail you your last paycheque once I figure out how much of it you actually earned."

"Oh yeah? You forget our little agreement from before? Don't think I won't go through with it. Your professor's named Gregory Hill, right?"

Christian's heart skipped a beat, the air freezing right out of his lungs, and then a better, stronger, couldn't-give-less-of-a-shit part of him smiled and nodded and said, "Yep. You want the number for his office? Because, you know, you'd actually be doing me a favour. If I get kicked out, it'll give me *way* more free time to cover all your and your little minion's shifts."

Melissa's mouth opened and closed, gaping like a fish out of water, and Christian *grinned* watching her flail and suffocate. Finally, she lifted her chin and narrowed her eyes, hands on her hips. "You know what? Fine. I don't need his number, 'cause I got his email." She swept her hair over her shoulder and stormed back to the door, whirling around at the last minute to shout, "You're gonna be fucking sorry you messed with me!"

"Feeling sorry already," he chirped back, and waved. "Bye now!"

Once she was gone, he started to shake. His whole body vibrated with adrenaline. His head spun. He couldn't get enough air into his lungs. God, he was going to vomit. Or faint. Or faint and vomit, and then asphyxiate.

Which would be okay, because his life was over, anyway. He could die now, or he could be a porn store employee for the rest of his life. Nobody else would want to hire him, not knowing where he used to work.

But then, if he died, they'd find his body on the floor of a porn store, surrounded by a puddle of pizza-vomit. Oh, Lord.

"You okay?"

He lifted his head from where he'd had it pillowed in his arms on the counter.

A customer peered at him from across the counter, concern written across his weathered face. One of the new regulars, an East Indian guy with a deep and abiding love of anal sex. The straight kind, specifically.

"I may need a paper bag," Christian said.

"You're looking kind of grey," the customer agreed. He handed Christian a DVD case.

"Oh, good. I must be dying. I was kind of hoping I'd die." He took the case, took note of the title—*Butt Sluts 7*, a classic—and spun his chair to the filing cabinets to find the disc. "So hey, if I do die, can you do me a favour and drag my body out into some back alley somewhere? I figure that's better than on the floor of a shithole porn store, right across from the twenty-five cent peep show booths."

The customer curled his nose, obviously offended. "Hey now! At least you get paid to be here. I'm coming into this 'shithole' of my own free will, so what's that make me?"

Christian sighed. "You're right. Sorry." What had Vicks told him during his interview? Damn, never mind Melissa, his attitude was going to sink this store all on its own.

"Ha! Just fucking with you, kid." The customer's face broke out in a huge grin. "I know I'm a pervert. I accept and embrace the fact that I love seeing a woman with two dicks up her ass. If that's wrong, I don't wanna be right."

Christian found the DVD he was looking for and scanned it and the guy's membership card into the rental system. "Yeah, you know what? I don't wanna be right either. *Fuck* right."

"That's the spirit!" The customer handed over his credit card, and once the transaction was complete, recited, "Due back Thursday," before Christian could get the chance to.

"Thanks, man, have a good one," Christian said to him as he left.

If this is wrong, I don't want to be right.

I don't want to be right.

I want to be happy.

He pulled out his cell phone and scrolled through his contacts. He'd hit dial on Max's number before he'd even decided what he was going to say. Or even whether calling Max was a good idea.

God, he should really do this in person.

Which he might have to do, because after five or six rings it was looking like Max was screening his call anyway. Which he totally deserved. He should just hang up. Right now. Riiiiight now. Riiiiiiiight—

"What."

Oh, God, he'd waited too long. Max had picked up and he was *pissed*.

"Christian. What."

Say something, you fucking idiot.

"I don't want to be right," Christian blurted.

"*What?*"

"I mean, um . . . if it means losing you, I don't want to be right. I mean . . ."

"Are you trying to say if being with me is wrong, you don't want to be right?" Still pissed, but now incredulous, too. The kind of angry where you just start laughing because there's no other response.

"No! Well, I do feel that way, and that's kind of what—"

"So you think it's wrong for us to be in a relationship? You think I'm the wrong guy for your image, is that what you're saying?"

"No. No, God no. I just mean . . . being right isn't worth losing you over. So I'm calling you to say I was wrong."

"But you still *think* you were right. You're just saying all this because you know it's what I want to hear."

"Argh, Max, stop trying so damn hard to stay mad at me! I'm saying it because I *was* wrong. Wrong to freak out at you. Wrong for letting the teacher thing go to my head until I thought *you* were wrong. Maybe even wrong about being a teacher in the first place, or at least maybe I'm being a teacher for the wrong reasons, I don't know."

". . . Go on."

Oh. Well. Christian hadn't expected that. It wasn't exactly an "I forgive you, Christian," and *definitely* not an "I forgive you, and I'm sorry, too, for calling you a half-black loser who doesn't care about his cancer-patient aunt," but it was an opening at least. Christian could work with that, assuming he could ever stop tripping over his own tongue. "Look, can I see you? Because I think you were a little bit wrong about me, too."

"Wow, so did you come up with that whole speech just to have an excuse to lay the guilt on at the end there? Pretty passive-aggressive."

"No! I just . . . I've been keeping a secret from you, too." God, he was really going to do this. He was really going to reveal to his saintly, secret-volunteer ex-boyfriend the fact that he worked in a job that literally included the daily task of mopping up cum from a twenty-five cent peep show booth. *I accept and embrace . . .* "It's pretty embarrassing, but I think it will put things into perspective. If you let it."

"I doubt that, but fine. Just promise me it really is embarrassing, not fake embarrassing like rom-com 'oh, I've secretly been a European prince the whole time!' embarrassing."

"Well, no, because that's the plot of *The Prince and Me*. But, in answer to your question, no, it's not fake embarrassing."

"Good. Just checking, because for a minute there I thought I was actually *in* a rom-com, with that 'If loving you is wrong, I don't want to be right' thing you just pulled."

"I didn't— Wait, wait, wait. Let me get this straight, here. So when you think 'rom-com,' your first thought is *The Prince and Me*? Not, I dunno, *The Princess Bride* or *Love, Actually* or *Ten Things I Hate About You* or . . . oh, I dunno, literally any other movie in the genre that doesn't completely suck?"

"Hey, remember the part where you're supposed to be grovelling? That doesn't include insulting my taste in Julia Stiles movies." Christian could almost *hear* Max smiling through the phone, but when he spoke again, it was in that same distant, pissed-off tone. "But sure. Okay, I'll come. I could use seeing you getting knocked down a peg."

"Oh, you'll see some pegging, all right. Meet me at 1081 Davie Street, okay? Just come right in."

"What is that, a restaurant or a coffee shop or something? It's not a gay bar, is it? Frankly I don't like you enough right now to do the bathroom hookup thing."

"It's not. You'll see."

Just as he hung up, a new email popped up in his inbox, *re: Illness in the family*. It was signed with Professor Hill's sprawling official

university signature, but the message itself was short and to the point:
Christian,
See me during my office hours ASAP.
Well, that was quick.

"A porn store?" Max asked as he walked in the door and spotted Christian standing there.

Christian had opted for Max's first impression not to be of him behind the desk, so he'd spent the last forty minutes wandering around straightening the shelves and re-alphabetizing the DVD cases—anything to stay on his feet and out in the open.

The moment Max had walked in, Christian rushed forward, arms out like they were going to hug. But Max's body language was closed off, arms folded around his body. His entire posture seemed to list backwards somewhat, as if he were being sucked toward the door by the vacuum of space. Christian's arms fell dejectedly to his sides, his face hot with embarrassment at his own enthusiasm and Max's rejection.

Max cast his eyes around the room, from the gang bang DVDs to the sex toys and back again. "What's your big secret, then? You have some kind of fetish? Man, it's not something to do with piss, is it?" His eyes narrowed as Christian mutely shook his head. "Or wait, let me guess, are you just one of those people with an addiction or a compulsion or whatever? Is that why you're so broke all the time?"

God, Max really was trying to stay angry at him, wasn't he?

"I work here, asshole," Christian finally snapped. "*This* is my aunt's business. The one that was going under. The one you said I should work at. Here I am." He spread his palms, gesturing expansively to the barely eighteen DVDs and the blow-up dolls and the glittery pink vibrators and even the peep show booths. *I accept and embrace . . .*

"Oh." Max's arms fell to his sides.

Now it was Christian's turn to cross *his* arms. "Yeah. 'Oh.'"

"*Ohhh.*"

This was starting to sound like the soundtrack to a porno. Time to get some dialogue in. "*Now* do you understand why I was so iffy about this job?"

Max blinked, staring around with freshly opened eyes, mouth gaping. "Your aunt. Owns a porn store."

"Yes."

"And you work here."

"I'm basically the manager, yes." Paused, furrowing his brow. "Actually, as of today, I'm the *only* employee."

That revelation didn't seem to land, because Max went on, "And you teach elementary school."

"Well, not yet, but that was the plan, yes."

"And you sell porn . . ." Max's gaze swung over to the shelf behind Christian's shoulder, the one he knew was for the barely eighteen stuff. ". . . of women in pigtails and school uniforms."

"Now you're getting it."

"And they're still letting you be a teacher? Letting you be around kids?"

"Probably not anymore. And please don't say it that way. I'm not . . ." *A pedophile.*

"Sorry. Wow. I'm still just . . . I'm still trying to wrap my head around the fact that my roommate who gets his fashion cues from Mr. Rogers works at a porn store."

Just your roommate? "Yes, well, you're the one who told me to rearrange my priorities."

"Wow, yeah, but when I said that I was thinking your aunt owned a used book store or a tourist shop down on Robson or something." He walked up and down the wall of toys, picked up a big dildo seemingly at random, gave it a cursory examination, and put it back again. He sniffed. "Do you seriously work here?"

"Yes. Seriously."

Max gave a distracted nod at that, and then abruptly stopped. He squinted. "Wait, what do you mean, 'Not anymore?'"

"I mean not anymore. That employee you overheard me talking to Rob about? She was blackmailing me to keep me from firing her. Well, I fired her."

"You seriously think she'll go through with it?"

"If the angry email I just got from my professor is any indication, then yes."

Max fell back against a wall of butt plugs, hand on his forehead. He looked dazed, like someone had just punched him in the jaw. "Shit. Sorry. Wow."

"Yeah."

For a while, they were both quiet, letting the reality of that sink in. Christian was getting kicked out of his program. All this time he'd been paranoid for a reason and now he was never going to become a teacher.

And why didn't that fact bother him more?

"So all this time, you've been working at a porn store? And keeping it a secret?"

"Well, yeah. It's pretty sensitive information, as you've seen. I was planning to tell you, though. On Halloween. That was before I learned that you're ten times the man I am."

"Huh?"

"Look, the whole teaching thing . . . I don't know, I like the idea of being a teacher, but I'm beginning to wonder if maybe I got into it for all the wrong reasons. Like, maybe I'm just doing it for approval." *My mother's approval, which I'll never, ever get. And I just need to accept that and get on with my damn life.* "And then there's you. You volunteer, do all this community service, but you keep it a secret. Because for you, it's not about the prestige or the image, it's about the actual good you do."

"Um . . . more like I keep it a secret because I don't want to end up being a self-righteous twat like my parents. And anyway, what do you mean, ten times the man you are? You took a job—at a place that could very likely get you kicked out of school—to help your sick aunt. And the whole time, you let me go on believing you were some kind of rule-obsessed, sweater-vest-wearing, judgmental little pencil-pushing—"

"Okay, I get the point."

"—coward." Max finished. "When, in fact, you're an absolutely normal person who takes a bit of time and encouragement to make a hard decision, but gets to the right choice in the end."

Christian's heart swelled, hearing that. Hearing that Max thought he'd done the right thing. He had no idea how much he'd *needed* to hear that until Max himself was standing there saying it. "Well you were right about some things. I *did* let this whole teacher thing change me. Man, I fucking *hate* sweater-vests. And ties. And khakis. The person who invented shoes that need to be polished can suck my dick, dammit. And yeah, I like to get fucking drunk sometimes, and if I want to do it at a bar, I shouldn't have to worry about some nosy helicopter parent seeing, and you know what else? As long as I'm not showing porn instead of Bill Nye to my classes, I don't fucking see how it's anybody's goddamn business what I do for a part-time job!"

"You are so hot right now," Max said. The lids of his eyes were low, shading the blown circles of his pupils. He slinked forward. Threw his arms around Christian's shoulders, drawing him close.

"Hwa?" Christian managed to say, just before Max's lips touched the corner of his mouth. And then they pressed again, right in the center, their mouths fitting together perfectly. Christian tensed up, then immediately relaxed again. Gave himself over to the kiss.

Just when it was getting good, though, Max pulled back. He pinched Christian's cheek, hard enough that bright pain flared under his skin. "You are a fucking idiot, Christian Blake. You seriously thought I'd look down on you for this? Well, guess what: I've never wanted you more. I *love* porn-manager you."

"You . . ."

Max smiled up at him, the expression paradoxically understanding and taunting. "Love you. Yeah."

"God, Max, I—"

"I'm not finished, Christian. This isn't some unconditional thing, so don't get all bigheaded. I love *this* version of you. Porn-store Christian. Christian with a chip on his shoulder. Christian who'd give up anything for his aunt." He stroked Christian's face, drawing Christian's gaze to him, then narrowed his eyes. *This is my serious face. Do you see how serious I am right now? Serious face.* "Stuck-up teacher Christian, on the other hand, I was kinda relieved to be breaking up with. You get me?"

Christian swallowed, his throat thick and dry, and he didn't know if it was fear or anticipation or tears coming on, or what. "So we *were* together, then? Before I fucked everything up, I mean? Boyfriends? Not just roommates?"

"Would I do *this*—" Max cupped Christian's cock through his jeans, right there in the middle of the store, and gave it a slow teasing squeeze. "—with a roommate?"

"I . . . oh God . . . I . . . I'd have to ask Noah to be sure."

Max's mouth touched Christian's neck now, an opened-mouthed kiss turning into a series of playful nips at his skin. "You do that. Later."

CHAPTER fourteen

m ax backed Christian up until he collided with a rack of DVDs, grabbed Christian's wrists and pinned them against the wire metal shelving to either side of his head. The whole structure rattled, a few cases falling to the floor at Christian's feet, but fuck it, because now Max was kissing him *hard*, filling every inch of his mouth with tongue. Christian twisted in that demanding grip, not enough to break free, just enough to cause friction between them, his chest and groin brushing Max's as he moved.

When he finally resurfaced from the mind-boggling pleasure of it all and opened his eyes, it was to the sight of a blow-up doll hanging in her package from a nearby wall, her big eyes staring into his own.

"Do you really . . ." He was unable to break eye contact with the doll. Max's hands were underneath his borrowed T-shirt, nails raking down his sides. He gasped, twisted, laughed a little. ". . . want to do this *here*?"

Max stopped his assault and looked up at Christian with another serious face. "You're absolutely right. Sex in a porn store? Who the hell would even think of such a thing? So inappropriate. Anyone who could pop a boner in *here* must be some kind of deviant—oh, what's this?" He tore down the zipper of Christian's jeans, mock scandalized at the sight of Christian's erection jutting through the opening. "And you're going commando, no less? Wow, porn-store Christian is fucking *filthy*."

Filthy deviant. Those words should have hurt him, but they just made him grin. *Yeah, I'm a filthy deviant. I work at a porn store and I'm gay and I have a huge boner for my boyfriend with a tongue ring. And I'm fucking happy.*

"Figured it was better than working in dirty underwear," he mumbled, but Max didn't seem hungry for an *explanation* as he lowered himself to his knees, palms on Christian's thighs and nose and mouth pressed to the hair at the base of Christian's shaft, breathing deep. "Oh. *Oh.*"

"You don't stink at all, in case you were wondering," Max said to his dick. He slowly jerked the shaft, then *finally fucking finally* ran the flat of his tongue up one side of it.

Christian's whole body arched upward. "I wasn't."

"You seem like the type to worry." Max twisted his wrist, spinning his palm around the base of Christian's shaft, and pulled the head of Christian's dick into his mouth.

Christian closed his eyes, biting his lip at the wet heat and the hard point of Max's tongue ring playing over his slit. "That was stuck-up teacher Christian," he gritted out. "This is porn-store Christian, and he's *nasty.*" To prove it, he grabbed both sides of Max's head and fucked into his mouth in one long stroke, not even stopping when Max let out a powerful gag. Christian would have pulled off if Max had struggled, but he didn't, just got two fistfuls of Christian's pants and held on for dear life as Christian rode his throat. He wouldn't last long like this, not long at all, already his ball sac was tightening, his pulse thrumming up the vein on the underside of his dick. "God, yeah, Max, God, God yeah—"

"Maybe I should come back later?"

Christian's eyes snapped open.

A customer was standing right in front of them: one half of the drunk couple that always came in for "personal recommendations." Shorter than his partner, he was bald and stocky and wore a goatee. And he was smiling flirtatiously, one eyebrow cocked, and making absolutely *no* effort to "come back later."

"Jesus!" Christian shouted, pushing Max off him and clapping both hands over his groin.

Max wasn't even remotely put off. He just sat back on his heels, erection clearly visible in his tight grey jeans, and wiped the back of his hand across his wet, reddened mouth. "Hi," he said. The roughness of his voice almost had Christian coming into his hands. "I'm Max."

"*Nice* to meet you, Max! I'm Terry." Terry's eyebrows were still up where his hairline would have been. He swung his gaze to Christian. "Didn't know you had a boyfriend, kid. And to think, my hubby was planning on asking you home with us next time we both came in."

Christian couldn't answer. Couldn't even begin to wrap his head around the *concept* of an appropriate response to that. He just made spluttering noises and tried to stuff his rock-hard dick back into the tiny little opening of his fly. How had it even gotten through there in the first place, that was what he wanted to know . . .

Terry's eyes twinkled. "So like I said, should I come back later?"

"Naw, man," Max said, still on his knees and seemingly not planning on getting up any time soon. "Customer comes first here at Rear Entrance Video—love that name, by the way—isn't that right, Christian?"

"R-right," Christian muttered. He finally wrangled his cock into submission and was able to zip his fly. His boner hadn't abated, even though by all rights it fucking should have. Something about the way Max was completely shameless . . .

"All right, then. Christian, I want to surprise my husband with a new plug. Do you have any suggestions?"

Max beamed up at him from his place on the floor. "Yeah, Christian, do you have any butt plug suggestions?"

Fucker, I'm going to make you regret this. "Sure," Christian said, awkwardly adjusting himself. "Let me show you."

Christian led the pair of them to the wall of sex toys, and went through the various options like a consummate professional. The whole time, he couldn't help but steal glances at Max, feeling electric tingles under his skin every time Max's lips parted or his pupils dilated or he took a sharp little breath. He found himself performing for Max's benefit, answering Terry's questions more candidly than he ever had before. Terry, for his part, was clearly enjoying himself, asking Christian what he thought of this girth versus that one, whether he thought that particular curve would feel good, if the vibrations on that particular model would be strong enough for Christian's tastes. No doubt he was going to *thoroughly* enjoy telling his husband about this later.

And even though this represented the first time Christian had felt fully comfortable with the job, maybe even *happy* with it, he was anxious for Terry to leave. He unabashedly sighed with relief when Terry finally chose a hot rod-red silicone plug with an optional vibrator—the first toy Christian had pointed out to him, *of course*— but Terry wasn't offended, he just smiled knowingly and tapped the side of his nose. "You boys have fun! Use a condom!" he said as Christian handed over his bag and receipt.

"You too!" Max replied, cheerful, then turned to Christian the minute he was gone and said, with a measure of urgency, "Okay, lock the door."

"Done fucking around?" Christian asked, trying to sound as nonchalant as possible. "Or should we wait and see who else wanders in? Maybe I can advise some drunk bachelorettes on the best vegetable-shaped novelty vibrator?"

"*Lock the door.*"

"Mmm." Christian's cock jerked and swelled when he heard the edge of desperation in Max's voice. Somewhere back there, Max had gone from teaser to teased, and Christian liked the frisson of tension that the role reversal inspired in him. He walked slowly up to the front door. Likewise slowly turned the deadbolt, and took even longer to hang the BACK IN FIFTEEN MINUTES sign.

He expected to turn and find Max panting for him, on his knees and ready to beg, but what he actually got was Max standing back, leaning coyly against a rack of DVDs with his hands tucked behind him. There was no mistaking the expression of pure mischief on his face.

Christian narrowed his eyes. "What."

Max pushed off the rack, hands still out of sight, and meandered toward Christian like they had all the time in the world. That was when Christian spotted the empty blister package still hanging on the wall.

"Max . . ." he warned, heart pounding.

"I was thinking." Max drew nearer and finally pulled his hand out from behind his back, presenting a row of bright pink anal beads that dangled from a ring around his index finger. Just the sight of them made Christian's hole clench, twin threads of anxiety and anticipation weaving through his entire body. "What's the fun of you working in a porn store if we don't take advantage of the perks?"

"Isn't having sex in one enough of a perk? Lotta guys—"

"Don't be a square, Christian. I'll pay for them."

"Damn straight you'll pay for them. But if you plan on *using* them"—*on me, I'm presuming*—"you'll pay for some lube and toy cleaner, too." He paused. "And I'm not giving you my employee discount, either."

"Sure, fine. Might as well add some condoms to my tab, as well. I didn't exactly come here expecting to get laid."

Yeah, tell me about it.

Max's expression faltered a little, and he cast Christian a searching look. "You are okay with this, aren't you, Christian? Because all teasing aside, if you're not—"

Christian stalked over to the neat display of lube bottles he'd so painstakingly set up a few weeks back. Snatched up a bottle, and pressed it into Max's hand. "Tell me how you want me," he said, and couldn't help the note of *Motherfucker, I can take whatever you can dish out* that came through in his growling tone.

Max's hand closed around the lube, his expression darkening. "Go take off your pants and lie on the floor, then."

God, Christian loved the sound of Max's voice when he was giving orders. Eager to follow them, he went to a clear space on the floor and undid his fly, hands shaking, while Max went to the counter where they kept a basket of condoms.

"You may want to keep your shoes on. Oh, and, ball up your pants and put them under your butt."

Heat flared through Christian's face. How could Max sound so chill about it all? He might as well have been giving Christian instructions on how to cut an onion. But as strange as it was for him, Christian still wanted to go along with it, still wanted to see what kind of new pleasures Max could show him.

He quickly stripped down and neatly rolled his pants into a pillow-shape, then bit the bullet and laid down on his back, planting the soles of his shoes against the floor and shoving his rolled pants under his ass. With his legs bent at the knee and spread, and his hips raised, he was completely exposed. Half naked and exposed on the floor of a porn store, and he fucking *loved* it.

"Damn." Max's gaze roamed up and down Christian's body. Every inch of Max screamed desire. Unlike Christian, though, he was still fully dressed, and didn't seem to be in too much of a rush to change that fact. He was holding the anal beads between his hands like a club he was planning on beating someone with.

Christian gulped.

Max must have seen that, because he dropped his threatening grip on the beads, letting them fall to his side, and said, "It's okay. I'll take it slow." True to his word, he slowly approached Christian, then carefully lowered himself to his knees between Christian's spread legs. Ran gentle hands up and down the trembling insides of Christian's thighs. When Christian didn't relax as instructed, he put on a mock look of disappointment. "Come on, porn-store Christian, where's your sense of adventure?"

Oh, fuck you, I am not *playing the shy virgin for you this time.* "Right here." Christian snatched Max by the wrist and pulled the hand with the anal beads up to his mouth, in the process yanking Max's entire body off-balance, until he was hanging overhead, parallel to Christian's body.

Christian held Max's startled gaze as he sucked the smallest bead of Max's—no, *their* new toy into his mouth. It was the size of a marble, perfectly round and silky soft. He didn't ask if Max had cleaned it, because that was something only stuck-up teacher Christian would concern himself with. Porn-store Christian, on the other hand, just trusted Max to take care of the details.

"Oh, baby!" Max groaned, biting his lip as he watched Christian work his lips and pull the second bead into his mouth alongside the first. The sensation of the beads in his mouth seemed to shoot straight to his balls. Maybe he could psychically convince Max to suck on those? "That is . . . that is hot. Hey, here, take this bottle of lube. You get these nice and wet for me using whatever . . . method . . . you prefer and I'll just . . ."

Christian was about to tease him about the fact that he couldn't even string together a sentence, when suddenly Max retreated down Christian's body, down until he was back between Christian's knees again, then lowered himself down to his elbows. Now it was Christian who probably couldn't string together a sentence. Max grinned up from behind Christian's jutting cock. Leaned in and blew a moist breath across Christian's sac.

Wow, I am psychic, Christian thought as Max sucked one of his balls into that hot wet mouth, and then all thought melted away as he drifted on sensations of mouth and teeth and tongue and spit. The sound of Max's muffled moans as he absolutely *devoured* Christian's balls, down to the sensitive skin between his legs and then—*oh fuck yes you brilliant bastard*—down to Christian's hole, where he fluttered and lapped and speared with his tongue and Christian was left helplessly howling around the mouthful of anal beads he'd been shamelessly taking in this entire time.

Max pulled back, and Christian whined with need as the cold air hit his spit-wet skin. "Lube," Max directed, out of breath. Christian handed Max the lube and then, to show he hadn't lost his nerve, passed over the anal beads, too.

His hole twitched, opening and closing again. He shut his eyes with a hiss as a frigid drizzle of lube ran across it. Kept them shut. "Do it."

Max kissed the inside of his thigh. "It's not a Band-Aid you have to rip off as fast as possible," he lectured, rubbing his hand in a slow circle over the place he'd kissed. Then he laughed. "Well, not *this* part."

Christian was still distracted, processing what that statement meant, when the first bead popped inside, his tongue-fucked hole taking it in easily. His cock twitched a little in interest. More lube drizzled down, and the second one was pretty easy to take, too. Christian kept his eyes tightly shut, focusing on the sensation of them inside him, the way his muscles held the different sizes. The third stretched him just slightly, not nearly enough for pain.

The fourth made him hiss, and then moan. Max just kissed his inner thigh again and nuzzled the skin.

The fifth hurt, but still passed easily enough; one second it was outside his body, and the next, it was inside.

The sixth took work on Max's part. He nudged and twisted it, slowly working it against Christian's hole, the entire string of beads spinning like a whirlpool, tracing him from the inside, and the sensation of that was so fucking new and amazing, he didn't really get the chance to notice the point when his hole opened around the widest part of the bead and then sucked up the rest behind it. He didn't even notice it had gone in until suddenly he was panting and sweaty with exertion.

"Feel good?" Max asked him.

Christian wasn't exactly sure, to be honest. Curious, he clenched around the strand, the motion seeming to tug the beads deeper. Yes, that did feel good. Very good. Unbidden, one of his hands wrapped around the base of his cock, and he gave himself a few frantic jerks, riding the feeling of all that strange movement and fullness, without the accompanying stretch of being penetrated by fingers or cock.

Suddenly, the beads moved back down toward his entrance again, working against the rhythm of Christian's body. Oh, Max must have his finger in the ring at the end. Using it, Max was pulling them down but not out. For now they stayed inside Christian's body, secure behind his clenched hole for as long as Max allowed.

As long as Max allowed.

Christian liked the sound of that, the idea that Max had such a pivotal role in his pleasure. Not that he was dependent on Max, or submissive to him, just that they were so deeply entwined.

Max's warmth disappeared from between his legs. Returned as a hot hand rolling a condom down Christian's shaft. And then cold again gradually turned warm as Max coated his dick in lube. There was the unmistakable sound of a pair of jeans falling to the floor. He wondered if he should open his eyes, see exactly what he was in for.

But he kept his eyes closed. He *liked* it, the way it exaggerated all sensations and blocked out the outside world—all the bare-shaven pussies and asses and cocks and women in pigtails that made up his surroundings—leaving him just with Max, Max's body and hands and warmth and breath. The beads shifting and rolling in his ass. Max's tight hole opening up around him as he lowered himself down onto Christian's dick.

"Jesus!" he shouted, hands flying up to cup Max's hips, which was when he discovered that Max was riding him *backwards*, crouched over his groin and facing his feet. Rocking forward and backward with one hand braced on Christian's knee. Taking Christian's cock at a completely unnatural but fucking *amazing* angle. God fuck, he wasn't going to last long like this.

"Tell me when you're going to come," Max said, and Christian must have answered him, because Max got back to work shortly after, taking every inch of Christian's cock up inside him, squeezing Christian's dick, and all the while the anal beads moved inside him, stroking his prostate, bringing him close, close, right—

"Now!" Christian said, and he didn't even know why, only that Max had asked him to.

No question. No hesitation. Max sat back on Christian's dick, reached between Christian's legs, and *yanked*.

The biggest beads popped out of him one at a time, and then the smaller ones all at once—the motion like ripping off a Band-Aid, Christian got the joke now—but as they flew out of Christian's body, they didn't hurt like a Band-Aid would. Instead, he felt a huge gusting relief and emptiness that turned the normally powerful pulsations of his dick as he came into a sideshow. He thrust his hips upward with a sound best described as a roar, gripping Max's waist hard as he emptied into him, never wanting to let go, never, never . . .

When he came around again, Max was kneeling by his head. At some point Christian had opened his eyes, because he could see Max's flushed face, Max's teeth biting down on his lower lip so hard that flushed pink turned white. Max's beautiful erect cock, foreskin sliding as he pumped himself to completion.

Without Max even asking, Christian opened his mouth and extended his tongue, happily accepting the jets of Max's cum as they fell. Swallowed. Smiled. Grabbed Max by the wrist and then the shoulder and pulled him down for a kiss. Felt sparks of pure pleasure and satisfaction all through his body when Max's tongue curled into his mouth.

Entwined.

CHAPTER fifteen

i t didn't take long to come back to the real world. Christian's back and knees ached, and from where he was lying, he was at the perfect vantage point to get an eyeful of Asian fetish videos. But even as the reality of what he'd done (and where he'd done it, good fucking God) came crashing around him, none of the usual guilt and misery followed. Instead, it was Max's hand reaching out for him. Max, with his jeans on but his fly undone, helping Christian to his feet with a smile and a kiss.

And then the store phone rang.

Christian kissed Max on the chin and shuffled, dick swinging, to the desk. Picked up the phone.

"Rear Entrance Video, Christian speaking, how may I help you?" He wondered if the person on the other end of the line would be able to hear the just-fucked-ness in his voice.

Max hopped up onto the counter beside him, watching Christian with a sated expression as he did up his fly and ran his hands through his mussed hair.

"Hi, Christian, it's Candace."

Oh, great. That didn't take long. Christian sighed, then forced himself to put a smile into his voice. "Hi, Candace, what's up?"

"I think you know."

He flashed Max an apologetic look. He really, really, *really* didn't want to have this conversation right now, especially since his balls were starting to get cold. Also, it was fucking humiliating. He didn't want to be this powerless on the best of days, and especially not in front of Max. "Let me guess: Melissa?"

"Yeah. I quit."

Not long at all. "Okay, thanks for calling. Have a good night."

Okay, thanks for calling?

Okay, thanks for fucking *calling?*

This girl was purposefully ruining his life, driving his aunt another step toward bankruptcy, and all he could say to her was *Okay, thanks for calling?*

Christian hit the End Call button, stared at the phone in disbelief a second, and then hurled it at the wall, where it shattered, batteries flying.

"O . . . kay," Max said. He slid off the edge of the desk and came to Christian's side. Gingerly took Christian by the arm. Christian had never seen him with such a sweet look of concern on his face. "Bad news? It's not . . . it's not your aunt, is it?"

"No, it's not—oh my God, my aunt! I haven't checked up on her all day!" Christian twisted out of Max's grip and dashed over to his discarded khakis. He wanted to be at the hospital *right now*, but the more seconds that passed, the more he realized how much was standing between him and his goal. The store was a mess. He needed to clean it up, close up shop, do the cash deposit . . .

"Christian. Talk to me. What's going on?"

Max was still standing by the counter, exactly where Christian had left him. Still with that same concerned look as before, but now it was tinged with sadness and confusion.

Open up to him. He's here.

"She's sick, Max. Well, I mean, she was sick before, but now—" Suddenly he was enfolded in Max's arms, his face pressed against the warmth of Max's neck. Hugging felt good, it felt so good, and only in Max's arms did he ever realize how starved for this he was. He sighed. Breathed deep. The fluttering panic in his chest faded to a low thrum, like a guitar string that had been plucked and plucked and plucked and now was being given time to slow down and go still.

At last he pulled away, although he kept a hand on Max's elbow. "She's been in the hospital the last couple of days. Pneumonia. She's unconscious and on a ventilator. I've been stopping by and visiting her whenever I can, but . . ." He shrugged and gestured to the store around him.

"You don't want her store to go under. I get it. Okay. Tell me what to do to help you. We'll close up here, and then we can stop by the hospital, okay? Together. You don't have to do this alone, Christian. Not anymore. Not as long as I'm here." He stood on tip-toes and kissed Christian on the nose, then padded over to the DVD rack they'd messed up and started picking up the DVDs and returning them to their proper places.

Christian, at a loss for words, just wandered back behind the counter and started counting out the till.

I'm not alone.

Even with the store slightly messier than usual thanks to their . . . exertions, with Max's help Christian was able to get it closed up in record time. Christian counted out the till and made the deposit while Max processed returns, filing DVDs and returning cases to their shelves, and mopped the floor. All the while Christian filled him in on the situation here, holding nothing back. About how he'd come here looking for a job, partially to prove Max wrong about him. About the store's financial problems. About how he'd quickly made enemies with Melissa, and the ways she'd been slowly dismantling the store. About her stealing from Christian and his aunt and their customers. About her blackmail and the resulting email from his professor. About Candace quitting in solidarity.

And then, when the bad stories were over, he told Max about saying "penis" during his interview, about Fabio the mannequin, about how Terry and his husband always tried to trick him into dirty talk, about the strange man who always came in wearing his slippers and rented only the most obscure and depraved titles the store had to offer. All the funny, ridiculous, unbelievable stories, the things he'd wished he had someone to talk about, but never had before. It felt good to hear Max laugh, or say "Ewww," or compliment him on Fabio's outfit.

It was like the hugs: he didn't know how much he'd been missing this connection until suddenly he had it, and he never wanted to let it go. He never wanted to let *Max* go.

"So you've been running this whole operation on your own?" Max said as Christian armed the alarm system and let him out the front door. "While going to school full time?"

Christian nodded. It sounded so much more . . . epic, almost *noble*, when Max said it.

All this time he'd been thinking he was some kind of irredeemable sleaze, a tainted person because he worked here, when in fact what he'd been doing was actually pretty great—selfless, even. God, he felt better and less conflicted about his motives for working at a porn store than he *ever* had about teaching.

Max had given him that. He smiled as he locked the door.

"No wonder you were such a touchy asshole this whole time," Max finished, and kissed him.

They sat together in the dimly lit front end of the bus, holding hands and watching the bright blurry shapes of passing neon in the rain. Christian felt warm and peaceful and so at ease with everything that he let his head fall on Max's shoulder and closed his eyes. Christian never slept on public transit after having his backpack stolen in tenth grade. And yet . . .

He woke to a squeeze around his hand and a kiss brushed against his forehead. "Isn't this our stop?" Max murmured into his hair, and Christian opened his sticky eyes. Yes, it was.

He stumbled to his feet as Max pulled the call bell. Was he awake, or was he sleepwalking? When the bus came to a stop, he tripped. Luckily, Max was there to catch him by the elbow and keep him upright, or else he'd have ended up flat on his face in a puddle.

"Christian, you're exhausted," Max said once they were safely on the sidewalk. A light misty rain hung around them, and Max's skin had a sheen under the streetlight. "How about we go home tonight, have a hot drink to warm up, and go see your aunt tomorrow? She's in stable condition, right? She'll be okay overnight. You need a rest."

Strange to have someone worrying about him. He'd always had his aunt for that, until she'd gotten sick and suddenly it was all Christian worrying about her. Kind of nice not to be the caretaker for once. Safe. Loved.

But no, as nice as that thought was, something was telling him to see his aunt *right now*. It was a stupid thing to think, he knew, but he felt like he was on the precipice of a transformation, that things in his life were falling into place.

Everything was changing. The store. Teaching school. Max. Christian's entire sense of self.

Why not his aunt, too?

He wished he could explain this in a way Max would understand, but he couldn't, so he just gave Max a wide-eyed look, gripped him by the shoulders, and said, "I have to see her, Max. I have a feeling."

Max didn't believe him; it was obvious in the way the corner of his mouth pulled, the way his gaze swung up to the streetlight. But he nodded. "Okay. Go in, see her. But you have to promise me you're going to come home to me afterwards. No more disappearing for days on end."

"You're not coming in with me?"

Max's mouth fell open. "Wh—no, I assumed you wouldn't—"

"I want you to. If you're okay with it, I want you to. I have this . . . I just feel like something's different now. Whatever it is, I want you to be there with me."

"Different doesn't necessarily mean good, Christian."

"I know. That's why I need you there."

"There's no taking this back."

"I know. Schrödinger's sick aunt." Christian barked out a weird, hysterical laugh at his own joke. The British may have made an art form of gallows humour, but out of Christian's mouth it felt slightly unhinged.

Max frowned and took Christian by the hand. "I meant *us*, Christian. Sorry if it sounds selfish, but if I go up there with you now, this can't be just sex anymore. Because whatever happens, however you respond, I'm not going to be able to fight loving you anymore."

"I don't want you to fight it," Christian told him, heart pounding, exhilarated and terrified. "I'm done fighting it myself."

They walked into the hospital hand in hand.

I'm sorry, but there's been no change in her condition.
Yes, I'm sure.
We'll call you if she wakes up. We have your number on file.
No, you'll have to come back during visiting hours.
"Come on, baby, let's get you home."

Christian remembered the sensation of drifting through space, the slow arcing turns, the hiss of bus doors opening and closing. Remembered Max's hand intertwined with his own, Max's nose touching the side of his face, Max's breath on his skin. Max leading him to the rickety stairs of their front porch, guiding him over that tricky first step, and then in through the front door and up the stairs to his room, where he was unwound from his soaking, cold jacket and stripped down, shirt and jeans and socks all laid over the radiator.

He got himself into bed—he wasn't a fucking invalid, dammit— and then Max was behind him, stripped to his underwear and just as clammy cold, pulling the blankets over both their shoulders. Shivering as he pressed to Christian for warmth. They stayed that way until the shaking stopped. Neither of them fell asleep.

The silence was terrible.

"It's not looking good for her, is it?" Max asked, tracing slow circles over Christian's shoulders.

"Same odds as a coin toss," Christian replied, and gave the darkness a broken smile. "Heads or tails, do you think?"

What if she died tonight, and he wasn't even there? What if she died, alone in that room, with tubes down her throat, all alone with no one to hold her and comfort her at the end? What would happen to her then? What would happen to *Christian*? He'd never forgive himself for that.

"Do you want to pray for her?"

"Wh—" Christian wrenched around, trying to turn and face him but just getting tangled in the sheets.

Max waited until he'd lain down and settled again, then continued. "I may not buy what my parents are selling, but I'm not going to pretend praying doesn't help. Although I will admit on that front that it probably helps *you* more than it does her."

"I just don't know what I'm going to do without her." He thought of Rear Entrance Video: about the fact that he'd been managing it for less than three months and under his watch it had lost every single employee, had hundreds of dollars disappear right under his nose, and now was on the verge of complete collapse. He could have saved the place from bankruptcy, given time, but not now. Not on his own. He had no idea what he was going to do now. Sell the business, he supposed. Hopefully he could get a fair price for a store with no steady clientele and no staff. Well, at least he could liquidate the stock . . .

He shook his head, wishing he could smack it against the wall but figuring Max probably wouldn't let him. "And God, here I am saying I don't know what to do without her and what I really mean is I don't know what I'm going to do with the *store* without her, even though she's the only damn family I have left. I'm a fucking wreck."

"You're taking care of her however you can, Christian. It's not the store itself that's important to you, it's the fact that it's *hers*. Everyone knows that. Everyone sees that. You're still a good person. Your heart's in the right place."

Christian rubbed his burning eyes. How could he be crying and smiling at the same time? "You're only saying that because you *have* to."

"Why, because you're my boyfriend now? Oh no. Trust me, that doesn't change a damn thing. You do dumb shit, I'm calling you out. Like tomorrow, for example. If I catch you in a sweater-vest after what you said tonight, I'm gonna . . . well, I haven't thought ahead that far yet."

"I still have to go to school tomorrow. I'm not kicked out just yet. Not officially." Christian sighed, still not quite sure how to feel about that. Numb, mostly. It was just too much all at once.

"Okay, I'm a fair man. *Tomorrow* you can wear a sweater-vest and a tie and the whole kit and kaboodle. Day after that, I want to see you in jeans and a T-shirt like a normal human being." He rubbed his knuckles into the top of Christian's head. "And don't worry about your aunt's store, okay? No *way* am I letting that tank."

Christian didn't see how that was possible, but even so, he couldn't help but admire Max's . . . faith? Maybe that was the wrong word, considering. Lack of fear? Determination? Whatever it was, Christian needed it. Bad.

Whatever happened tomorrow, with his school, with the store, with his aunt lying alone in hospital . . . It was like standing on the edge of a black hole.

"We're going to get through this, Christian." Max kissed the back of his neck. "Together. You'll see."

God, he hoped so.

In the morning, he called Vicks, explained what had happened with Melissa and Candace, and begged her to take the dayshift, promising he'd be there to take over as soon as he'd finished his meeting with his professor.

"And after today?" Vicks asked. "This baby is *coming*, Christian. Well, not today or anything, as far as I know, but soon. I am a ticking time bomb, you get me? And there is no damn way I'm working the counter with a kid on my tit."

"You won't have to," Christian whispered into his phone as he scanned the floor for a presentable-looking pair of pants to wear. Max was still asleep in the bed, sprawled out on his belly and taking up every last inch of space. Hogging all the blankets, too. "After today, school won't be an issue anymore, okay? I'll be available 24/7."

"Okay, that's great, but you can't *be* there 24/7. You're a human being, Christian, not a machine."

"I know. I'll find some new hires, even if I have to find some stoners as a Band-Aid solution, or I'll change the store hours, or something. I'll handle it. I just need you today. Pleeeeeease."

She grumbled. "Fine. But when you show up for shift change, bring me a ginormous Green Tea Frappuccino. And a cheeseburger. From Vera's. No fast food shit. And go to that cupcake place on Denman and get me a piña colada cupcake."

"Okay. Got it. It's all yours." Christian stepped into his pants and wiggled them up until they were on his waist. He did up his fly. "One venti Green Tea—"

"No, wait, you know what, that's what I'm craving *now*. Call me when you're on your way for up-to-date instructions."

"Call you. Okay. Thanks. I owe you."

"Yes, you do. Now let me go back to bed for a few more hours."

Christian hung up and finished dressing. The whole time, Max slept on, although at some point he'd pulled a pillow up over his head. *Lazy shit.* And yet, rather than feeling annoyed like he once would have, Christian just smiled fondly. *Yeah, well, now he's my lazy shit.*

He didn't see how Max could pull through on all of last night's grand promises, but maybe that didn't matter. Maybe just having Max there with him while the whole world went to pieces would be enough.

It'd have to be, after today. Christian checked himself in the mirror behind his door, straightened his tie with a nod of self-approval, and slipped out of the room.

This was it.

CHAPTER sixteen

there was no point in going to class, so Christian used his dubiously earned free time to stop by the hospital, during visiting hours for once.

His aunt was still unconscious, but Christian spent an hour or so by her side anyway, holding her limp hand and telling her about his last couple of days. The store. Max. Teaching school. How he was going to get kicked out of it in . . . oh, about two hours.

Near the end of his visit, Sandra arrived with a huge bouquet of rainbow balloons, and when she saw Christian looking, said, "There's a ban on *flowers*. I didn't see anything about balloons, so fuck it. This place is goddamn depressing. No wonder she won't wake up."

They hugged when he left.

He thought he'd be more anxious on the bus ride up to campus, but instead he was strangely calm. Maybe this was how it felt to be the kind of person who, sentenced to death and about to be executed, whipped out a quotable destined-to-be-immortal bon mot instead of *Please don't kill me I'm too young to die.*

The truth was, since firing Melissa, every second that passed got him closer to accepting the fact that he didn't *need* to be a teacher. He had no doubt he was still a do-gooder—he wasn't exactly about to resign his life to 24/7 World of Warcraft, at least—but it didn't have to be teaching anymore. There were lots of things he could do to contribute to the world and not compromise so much on who he was. Maybe Max could get him some work in the Downtown East Side. After all, it didn't seem too likely that addicts would give a shit that he part-timed at a porn store. He could staff a suicide hotline for gay teens. He could work at a (non-religious) food bank. The possibilities were endless. It had taken facing down a dead end to realize that.

He'd never felt so free. He walked into his professor's office with his head held high.

Professor Hill's office was the typical hole-in-the-wall, a small room with a desk and a couple of chairs and walls lined with books and binders. He also had a pretty substantial art collection, all crayons and markers, clearly from children under the age of ten. The man himself was seated behind a desk piled high with paperwork. He didn't look up from his grading, instead waving Christian into a seat across from his desk. "Christian," he said, eyes still on his papers. "Thanks for coming in."

"No problem," Christian replied, not sure what else to say. *Thanks for kicking me out of the program in person?*

"So, I'm hoping you already know why I've asked you in today."

"Yes, sir."

"And you know it's serious."

"Yes, sir."

"And you understand our policies on expelling students, which I went over with the class earlier in the year."

"Yes, sir."

Finally Professor Hill looked up, steepling his hands and peering at Christian through his rimless glasses. "Okay. So in light of all that, do you have a good reason why you're missing class and handing in assignments late?"

"Yes, sir."

Wait, what?

"Let's hear it, then." Professor Hill took off his glasses and primly folded them on his desk, looking up at Christian again with clear, compassionate eyes. "I know you and I haven't really gotten along so far this semester, but that doesn't mean I'm not willing to hear you out if there are extenuating circumstances." *What? What? What?* "Because despite your poor performance the last few weeks, you were a model student at the start of the semester, and after looking over your application and volunteering record, I really do think you have a lot of potential as a teacher. I don't want to act rashly and miss out on that."

This isn't about the porn store? This isn't about Melissa?

Christian scrambled to come up with a suitable reply. "Thank you for saying so, sir. And I'm . . . I'm glad you're giving me a chance to explain myself." *So explain yourself. Come on. Say something!* "And my good reason is . . . well . . . it's just . . . It's like my email to you said. My aunt has been sick, sir. She has ovarian cancer, you see, and I'm . . . well, I guess I'm her next of kin. My mother—her sister—lives in Jamaica, and so do their parents. She has a roommate to act as her caretaker at home, but she has a full-time job and isn't related to her like I am, you know? My aunt is also a small business owner, so I've been trying to keep that afloat for her, and now she's in the hospital and—" His throat felt thick, choked. He wished for some of that calm he'd been feeling on the way up here, but so far it was eluding him.

Professor Hill nodded sombrely. "You could have told me that earlier, Christian. We do have systems in place for students to take a semester off without penalty when it comes to extenuating circumstances such as these."

"Oh."

"But then, I suppose I could have asked earlier, too. You've had a lot on your plate, it's not hard to see why you wouldn't prioritize keeping me in the loop."

"Yeah, I guess."

"So here's what I want you to do, Christian." Professor Hill bent for a moment, dug through his desk drawers, and pulled out a couple of photocopied sheets. He slid them across the desk to Christian. "I want you to take these forms, fill them out, get them signed off by your aunt's doctor or whoever at the hospital handles that kind of thing. Then I want you to submit them to Student Services and take the rest of the semester off, until things in your life calm down. Next semester, if you're ready to come back, email me, and I'll find you a practicum placement with everyone else. You'll still have to complete your coursework semester, but you can do that next fall. You'll be behind your classmates graduating, but all going well, you'll have your teaching certificate by the January after next."

"Really? It's that easy?" He wished he'd known that earlier, rather than listening to the hype about limited space and high competition that made him believe if he took time off, his space in the program would be given away to someone more worthy.

"If you want it to be. If this is what you want, we can make it happen. *Is* this what you want, Christian?"

Is this what I want? God, I never thought I had a choice.

Professor Hill was watching him. Scrutinizing him. Even if he wasn't speaking, he was giving *some* kind of answer in his expression. Too bad Christian himself didn't know what that answer was.

Finally, without really thinking, some words fell out of his mouth. "It is, but . . ."

"But what?"

Suddenly he knew exactly what it was he wanted to say. What he'd *always* wanted to say. "But I don't want to change who I am."

Professor Hill blinked, an expression Christian interpreted as incredulous confusion.

"I can keep my nose clean on Facebook, Professor Hill, and I can spend forty hours a week in a tie even if it's frankly kind of ridiculous—sorry, professor—but I can't . . . I can't . . ." He balled his hands into fists. "I'm gay, Professor Hill, and I have a boyfriend I really love, and I can't hide it anymore. And if that means I can't be a teacher—"

He thought Professor Hill might laugh dismissively or turn red with fury and call him a child predator, but he just nodded again. "I understand your concern."

"You do?"

"Yes, I do. I'm not gay myself, but you're hardly my first LGBT student, Christian." He flashed a tight smile. "I can't promise it will never be an issue for you, especially when it comes to parents, but I can promise to make sure you're placed in a school with administrators who are willing to go to bat for you if somebody *makes* it a problem."

Christian was stunned, feeling like a bird who'd flown into a window. He realized belatedly that out of all the lectures on conduct and three strikes and ties and Facebook and alcohol use, nobody had *ever* mentioned sexuality, not even once. He'd just inserted that bit on his own. Well, maybe some of the credit for that belonged to his mother and all the psychological damage she'd inflicted. "Oh. Uh, then . . . Thank you."

"You're welcome. So, those forms?"

Christian took them, folded them crisply in half, and stuffed them into his satchel. "Yes, sir."

"I hope your aunt gets better soon and that you're able to come back in January."

"Thanks," Christian said. "Me too."

And then, still in shock, not even sure yet if he really *did* want to come back in January, he got up, shook Professor Hill's hand, and walked out.

CONGRATULATIONS! read the banner hanging over the New Releases rack.

Christian stared up at it in confusion for a second or so until someone came flying at him from the direction of the counter and tackled him into the wall of sex toys.

Max?

Well, he was getting kissed all over the face, so if it *wasn't* Max, he was in trouble.

"Surprise!" Max said.

"Surprise!" someone—no, several other someones—echoed. Four voices. All guys.

His roommates appeared from behind various DVD racks one by one. Rob. Noah. Austin.

Christian looked to Max in terror, expression likely screaming *What have you fucking done?* But then he realized. His roommates were all smiling. They didn't care that they were in a porn store. They probably knew why Christian was here, too. They didn't care.

"What's all this?" he asked, when Max finally unwound Christian from his wiry arms.

"It's your congratulations-on-not-being-a-square party," Max said, gesturing expansively to the store. There were balloons tied to the racks, and Vicks was sitting behind the desk, already started on the first of three pizzas.

"So you guys . . . you guys all know?" Christian asked, still not quite able to get over that single fact.

"Max filled us in," Rob said with a nod. "Sorry about your aunt."

"Yeah, sorry," Noah echoed. "But remember when I said I'd help you with whatever you needed? Here we are."

"Wh—" Christian looked between them, from face to smiling face, feeling like the meaning of all this was just beyond his grasp, like a word on the tip of his tongue.

"Oh, yeah," Max said. "It's also a congratulations-on-your-store-not-closing-down-because-now-you-have-a-staff party."

"I have a staff?" Christian asked. He looked to Vicks helplessly.

She shrugged and took another bite of her pizza.

Austin punched him in the shoulder. "Yeah, you idiot. Us."

"You?"

"Yes. Us." Max looped a hand around Christian's elbow and led him to the counter, to a brand new employee schedule. Christian read the names down the left-hand side: Christian. Max. Rob. Austin. Noah. "I came here as soon as you left this morning," Max explained. "Met Vicks here and told her to train me. I'm pretty much ready to start working on my own, although you'll need to come in to do the cash deposits. Sorry."

According to the new schedule, Christian still had the weeknight shifts he'd been working, but now it was a manageable four nights a week, Monday to Thursday, with the rest of the shifts divvied up between his roommates.

"I talked it over with Chef," Noah said. "As long as I do prep during the week, he's okay with me showing up at the last minute before dinner service on Sundays and Mondays, at least until you find some new staff. He says sorry about your aunt."

"I only have classes three days a week and practice is in the evenings," Austin added. "So I'm good. Actually, more than good. Free porn. Yes. Score."

"I've never heard of an all-dude porn store before, but as long as it means I get my maternity leave, I really don't give a shit." Vicks reached forward for another piece of pizza, then flicked her gaze to Christian. "You still owe me that Frappuccino, by the way. Don't think I didn't notice you never called me like you *said* you would. You're just lucky your boyfriend here brought pizza." She took a bite, closing her eyes and absolutely savouring it. "Even though it's gonna give me heartburn. Hurts so good."

Max came up behind Christian and rubbed his shoulders. "See?" he said into Christian's ear, the gust of his breath soft and sweet. "I told you it would be all right. Do I get a thank-you kiss now?"

Christian spun in his arms and planted one right on his mouth.

"Get a room!" Austin shouted, and then laughed at his own joke.

It was the happiest Christian could ever remember being. He broke off the kiss, looking proudly from face to smiling face. His *friends*, who'd come through for him against his every expectation, standing around him now in celebration. "The good news isn't over, either," he announced. "I met with my professor and I'm not getting kicked out of my program! I still get to be a teacher!"

"Awesome! Congratulations!" Rob cheered, and Austin clapped him on the back. The good feeling in his chest swelled bigger and bigger and bigger, threatening to burst.

"Oh," Max said. "Oh, um . . . congratulations, Christian. That's great. I guess."

And burst it did.

But when he looked to Max for an explanation, he was smiling the same as ever as he held out a can of pop in offering. But Christian *knew* he hadn't imagined the strange hurt in Max's voice. And he wasn't imagining the shuttered expression in Max's eyes, either. Everyone was watching them, though, so Christian couldn't ask him what was wrong.

Instead, he just took the can of pop, cracked it open, and raised it in a toast. "To Rear Entrance Video," he said, and then, voice shaking a little, "And to Auntie Beverly."

It was Rob who took Christian's hand, then, and gave it a gentle squeeze. "To Christian's not-so-deep-dark secret," he said and raised his drink, flashing Christian a fortifying smile.

Austin was the last one to toast, grinning from ear to ear as he did. "To free porn!"

Christian watched Max all night. Watched him eat pizza with Noah and try out strap-ons for Austin and steer a foamy-mouthed Rob away from the creepiest of the Asian fetish videos. Watched him smile and laugh and even rent out a couple of DVDs to a slightly mystified customer who couldn't seem to wrap his head around the fact that there were more than two people in the store at one time.

He seemed normal, mostly. As much of a shithead and a flirt and a lackadaisical charmer as he ever was, except for a couple of moments when he thought nobody was looking, when Rob's head was turned or Noah was flirting with Vicks, and then his eyes would get a distant look and he'd frown a little. And then the moment would pass and he'd be smiling again.

At the end of the night, Christian closed up the store and they all took the bus home. Austin plopped down in between Max and Christian, and Rob and Noah sat together across the aisle, Rob immediately nodding off on Noah's shoulder. Nobody spoke. Maybe it was supposed to be a sleepy, companionable silence, but for Christian, at least, it wasn't.

He desperately wanted to talk to Max about whatever it was, but Max didn't seem too interested in talking to *him*. Every perfectly innocent attempt at conversation that Christian tried to make ended with a monosyllabic answer, and when they got home, Max immediately trudged up the stairs and disappeared into his room, as if he didn't even want Christian to follow.

Well, fuck that noise.

Christian slipped in behind him and clicked the door shut. Max had his back turned, and his shoulders were tense. All signs pointed to him being about to kick Christian out.

What the fuck is your problem? Christian wanted to ask, but said, "Is there something we need to talk about?" instead. Calm voice. Not too confrontational. Teacher Christian, back again.

Max spun to face him, and his lip was curled as if Christian really *had* just asked him what the fuck his problem was, but then his face fell and softened and he sat on the bed, patting the space beside him.

Christian sat.

Max stared down at his folded hands. "Christian, look, I really . . . I really, really like you, but this isn't going to work out."

"What? What isn't going to work out, Max?"

He asked that, but he had a pretty damn good idea. An idea that Max quickly confirmed: "You. Us. I'll still work at your aunt's store, I'm good for it, but I can't be your boyfriend."

And even though he'd suspected it, it still fucking hurt like a hammer to the chest to hear, and it knocked the wind out of him just the same. "Wh—why—but—" God, wasn't it five hours ago Max had asked him for a thank-you kiss, and twenty-four hours ago had told Christian he loved him? What had changed?

Oh.

"This is about me not getting kicked out of my program, isn't it? You only wanted to date me when I was"—*a loser like you*—"free of all that. Well listen, let's talk about this." If it sounded like begging, that's because it was. "It's not going to be like it was before, Max. I'm not going back into the closet, and I'm not ditching my aunt's store. I'm not going to throw you away, and you know what, my prof knows I'm gay and that I have a boyfriend and he doesn't care. I said I wasn't going to rejoin the program if I couldn't be with you. He agreed, Max. It's okay. I can have b—"

"Jesus, Christian, I wish it was that simple. I really do, but it's not. I . . ."

Christian grabbed Max by the shoulders and forcibly turned him so they were face-to-face. Pressed a kiss to his cheekbone. "It is, Max. It really is. I'm sorry for how I treated you before, I really was a fucking coward, but it's going to be better this time. I'm not going to hurt you like that again. I'm still going to try being a teacher, but it doesn't change the fact that I'm yours, one hundred percent. I love you."

Max still wouldn't meet Christian's eyes. He twisted his shoulders half-heartedly, not rough enough to free himself, but enough to show Christian he didn't want to be touched. Christian's hands fell to his sides.

"And I love you, Christian, and that's why I have to do this. It's— fuck, I can't believe I'm saying this—it's not you. It's me. This is all me. I thought I could—well, I don't know what the fuck I was thinking. I thought I could pretend to be someone else. You have this vision of me as this selfless volunteer and I thought I could be that person, for you at least, but I can't lie to you that way, and now that you're still going to be a teacher, it's either lie or let you go. God, I'm such a fucking hypocrite."

His eyes kept flickering to his computer, to the screensaver of the shirtless woman wading in tropical shallows.

"What?" Christian asked, and this time he couldn't keep the confrontational tone out of his voice. "What is it? You're closeted yourself? You—you have a girlfriend? You have a criminal record? You have an STD? Because I don't care about that. You really are going back to Christ?"

"No!" Max frowned and twisted like he was being tortured, and then a fierceness came into his eyes, an expression that said, in all fucking seriousness, *You want the truth? You can't handle the truth.* "No. It's not that. You want to—you really want to know what it is? Well, here goes, Christian. You know how I'm broke most of the time, but then sometimes I just have a ton of cash?"

"Yeah, and you buy us all pizza and beer. What—oh shit, you're actually a drug dealer, aren't you?"

Max scoffed. "I work with *addicts*, you fucking idiot! Of course I'm not a goddamn dealer, what kind of asshole do you think I am? Jesus!"

"Oh. Well." The shame of that accusation was heavy enough that Christian had to fight the urge to hang his head. It was like a physical weight pulling him down. When he spoke again, it was soft, apologetic, barely above a whisper. Christian wasn't Catholic, but he imagined this must be what confession felt like. "I don't think you're an asshole, Max. I just don't understand. Help me. Please."

Max looked like he was practically in tears. "Fine! You know what, Christian? Fine. I'll show you." He stormed across the small space to his desk and gave his computer mouse a couple of angry clicks. "You may want to shift a foot or so to the left," he snarled over his shoulder.

Too confused and frankly intimidated by Max's demeanour to protest, Christian moved.

A white pop-up appeared in the center of Max's computer screen: a chat room, by the looks of it, with a huge black square in the top left hand corner. Suddenly the green light of Max's webcam turned on, and the black square turned into a picture. Max's room. Max's bed, right where Christian had been sitting before he'd shifted to the left. Max was still well in view, though.

No sooner had the webcam picture appeared, several messages showed up in the chat room half of the window. Christian had to squint to see the tiny letters.

hey ;)
Hey sexy, private room?
hi u btm
see yr abs?
Oh.

CHAPTER seventeen

m ax waited patiently for Christian to finish reading, arms crossed over his chest. When Christian sat back again, he spread them expansively and said, "Now do you get it? *This* is who I am. This is how I get my money. I jerk off and flex my muscles and fuck myself with a big dildo and eat my own cum and once a month I get a check—occasionally a big one—in the mail."

Christian was still processing what he was seeing, still trying to wrap his mind around the thought of Max sitting down here, naked or in his Spider-Man underwear—God, everything a performance, all of it so carefully calculated—flirting with the men on the other side of this screen, letting them tell him how to touch himself, what to show of himself, what to—

Max Xed out the window and sat down on the bed again, just out of Christian's reach. "I kept trying to decide if I should tell you, or break up with you, or quit doing it, or just do it behind your back . . . I felt like *shit*, Christian. But then I thought, well, once you relaxed on the whole perfect-teacher-image thing, maybe I *could* tell you and we could just figure it out from there as a couple, but now you're still a teacher and you're trying to do right by me and I'm fucking everything up. This could fuck up your whole life, Christian. Maybe you can get away with being gay, but having sex with a fucking camwhore? *Dating* one?" He scrubbed his face with both hands. "If you got kicked out because of me you'd hate me, and I'd hate myself. If you didn't get kicked out, you'd constantly be worrying about it and you'd resent me for making you worry, but if I just quit, I'd resent *you* and I'd think you were secretly judging me . . ."

"Let's talk about it, then," Christian said. "I want to talk about it. How about *both* of us stop doing what we think is best for the other person and actually ask what they think is best for them?"

"Okay," Max murmured. He didn't take his face out of his hands, but at least it was a start. An opening.

Christian reached out and cupped Max's shoulder, relieved when Max didn't shrug him off again. "So, yeah," he started. "I'm a little upset. Not because of what you're doing, but because you thought you had to keep it a secret from me. I know I act a little uptight—" Max lifted his head at that, flashing Christian an incredulous look. "Okay, a lot uptight. But that's *me*. That's my life and my image and my compromise to make. I wouldn't ask anything like that of you. And I'm not jealous, either. If we're going to be boyfriends, yeah, I want to be monogamous, but I don't own you, and I don't own your body, and just because you have a boner doesn't mean it isn't still work. What you and I do together is completely separate from that."

"C'mon, Christian. You say that—and thank you for being cool about it, it really does mean a lot to me—but that doesn't change the fact that what I do endangers your career."

"So does the porn store, Max. Just because I managed to avoid getting booted this time doesn't mean I'm out of the weeds. Anybody finds out, anybody complains, I'm toast." Saying it aloud filled him with a lancing fear, but a determination, too. "But I don't care about that risk, because I'm doing it for my aunt. My aunt, who's worth *anything*, even having to give up on my dream. Wasn't it you who lectured me about 'priorities'?"

Max barked out a laugh, a single hoarse *Ha!* that betrayed the fact that he was on the verge of tears. "I guess I was. But that's different, Christian. She's family. I—"

"And I want *you* to be family, Max. I said I loved you, and I meant it. You're worth it too."

"Bullshit."

"Not bullshit."

"Dude, I don't want to be the one to cost you your dream of teaching. I just don't. Don't put that on me."

Christian wanted to roar with frustration, but instead he just took Max by the chin and looked into his eyes. "I'm not putting it on you. You're not responsible for me, Max, any more than my aunt is. I mean, when you thought I was getting kicked out, did you blame her for it? Were you mad at her?"

"Uh, no, I guess not," Max mumbled, gaze slipping to one side. "I was kind of thankful, actually."

"Exactly. So look, quit the self-sacrifice, because that's my bag. I'm a big boy. I can make my own decisions about what—and *who*—is important enough for me to risk my chance of being a teacher, and I'll prove it to you right now. Turn on your cam again."

"What? No!"

"Do it! It's got a filter that lets you blacklist certain cities and IPs, right?"

Max nodded numbly. "I already have the entire lower mainland blocked. And my parents back in Alberta."

"So do it!" Christian said, and before he could second-guess himself, stripped off his sweater-vest and shirt.

"What are you— Oh my God, Christian, you can't be serious."

"Dead serious. Turn the cam on." Christian stepped out of his pants.

Over on the computer screen, the webcam window flickered to life, the image showing Max's bewildered face and Christian's torso and half-hard cock in his geeky white boxers.

Several chats popped up nearly instantly.

got a friend tonite?
who's your boyfriend
suck his cock
private???

Christian forced himself to stop looking at the screen. This wasn't about the men on the other side. It was about *Max*.

Max, who was hunched over the computer typing something back as he combed a hand through his hair in a gesture simultaneously flirtatious and anxious. "I'm going to turn the sound on now," he said. "They're going to be able to hear us, but we're not going to be able to hear them. If you don't want them to see your face, just stay standing like you are. You sure you want to do this? *Absolutely certain?*"

Christian's heart pounded. Last chance—no. He was doing this. For Max. For both of them. He cleared his throat. "As long as I get half the money for the show, then yeah, I'm sure."

"We can negotiate rates later," Max replied, trying to match Christian's glib tone and failing just as badly as Christian had. He was nervous too, which made Christian feel a little bit better about his own uncertainties.

Another couple taps on his mouse, and when Max spoke again, something had changed in his voice. It was that same flirtatious growl he used on Christian, but more clearly pronounced, this voice to his actual sex-speak as a stage whisper might be to a real one. "Hey guys! Guess who decided to stop by? This is my roommate . . ."

"Blake," Christian finished, keeping his voice low.

"Blake, yeah." Max looked to Christian and gave him an encouraging nod, then turned back to the camera. The image of him on the screen bit his lip and lowered his eyelids. "He just moved in— Why don't you ask *him* if he's gay or not? Blake?"

Christian tried to think of porn he'd watched, and what Max's viewers would prefer to hear. "I'm . . ." He cleared his throat. Lowered his voice again. Deeper. Meaner. "I'm straight. But a blowjob's a blowjob, isn't that right, Max? That's what he's been telling me every time he begs to get his lips around my dick."

Max on the screen licked his full lips obscenely, and even though Christian knew the performance wasn't for *him*, it still made his cock twitch and rise. He could see it in the webcam: big and thick, tenting his white boxers and pointing right at Max's cheek. Possessed by the weird thrill of seeing himself this way—disembodied, just a cock and a voice, an object of desire and envy—he thrust his hips, bumping the rigid length of his erection up one side of Max's face.

A moment of genuineness in the midst of the performance as Max laughed in surprise, and then he turned, serious again, and ran his palms up the front of Christian's thighs until his hands framed Christian's cock and pulled the fabric around it taut. He turned up adoring eyes, and even Christian couldn't tell if the expression was real or for show. Maybe it was both, Christian thought as Max pressed an open-mouthed kiss to the underside of his shaft through the fabric.

"Strip," he commanded gruffly, remembering himself.

"Hell yeah, daddy-o." Max grinned and peeled off his shirt, turning three-quarters to the camera and subtly flexing his pecs and abs as he did. It was pretty damn sexy. Christian could definitely believe guys paid to see him in action.

And I get the real deal.

When it came time to take off his pants, Max stood and turned his back on the camera, giving his viewers a booty shake in his—good Lord—*Captain America* underwear. "And yes, before you ask, I do have all of the Avengers," he said to Christian with a wink, and bent forward, hooking his thumbs in the waistband of his underwear and tugging them just below the curve of his ass. Settling the top half of his body on his bed, he looked to Christian in invitation.

Christian looked into the computer screen and watched himself as he traced down the crevice of Max's crack with three fingers, poking just the tip of the middle one into Max's hole on the way by. Max's pained little moan at the penetration wasn't *remotely* faked. It set Christian's blood on fire.

"Should I spank this fine ass?" Christian asked the camera.

Their chat room went wild.

fuck yeah

y

Yes

YES!!

yesyesyes

Max gave a teasing little wiggle to the camera at the same time as he gave Christian a barely noticeable nod of permission. It was all Christian needed; he wasn't about to wait for Max to beg. So he lifted his cupped palm and brought it down on Max's left ass cheek with a loud, incredibly satisfying SMACK. And again, this time on the right side. The left. He paused for a second after that, rubbing Max's hot skin. "More okay?" he whispered. "Am I doing okay?"

The answering smile was almost a grimace, but it was still a yes.

"Should I give him more?" Christian asked the camera in his booming straight guy voice.

Another stream of *yes*es flooded in.

Christian obliged them, trying to find the perfect balance between making the impact loud for their viewers and not actually hurting Max. Which was a kind of hard line to judge, now that Max was yelping like he was being whaled on with a studded belt versus getting little love taps from his boyfriend.

"Yeah, you all know he deserves it," Christian said, monologuing like a supervillain, mostly to give Max (and his own arm) a break. "I mean, look at this slut, begging to blow his straight roommate. What do you guys think, am I the first roommate to get a BJ from this whore mouth?"

He didn't bother squinting to look at the answers that popped up in quick succession. He knew exactly what they'd say.

"Well, if that's the case, no way am I sticking it in *there*." Max rolled his eyes. Okay, maybe Christian was laying it on a little thick. "On the other hand . . . I bet I *am* the first straight guy to be horny and hard up enough to fuck this tight ass. I mean, if a blowjob's a blowjob then a hole's a hole, right?"

He went off in search of lube and condoms, leaving Max to entertain his adoring public. Said entertainment consisted mostly of dirty talk—much of it commenting on how hot Christian was, how hungry Max's hole was for that big dick, how horny he was to have them watching—while Christian scrambled out of his boxers and rolled a condom down his erection, which despite his nervousness wasn't remotely close to flagging. The dirty talk probably helped with that. Even though it wasn't directed at him, Christian couldn't help but enjoy it, not just the words themselves but the breathless growl Max spoke in. He could listen to that all day and not get bored, although he'd probably start to chafe sooner or later.

Speaking of which, time to stop stalling and do this thing. Give Max what he was clearly begging for with his ass in the air as he bent forward over his keyboard. Christian took a deep breath and stepped back into the frame. Leading with his dick. Max-on-the-computer's eyes widened. A pleased Cheshire Cat smile crept across his face. He licked his lips again, but this time it definitely wasn't for show.

It likewise wasn't for show when Christian grabbed him by the hair and yanked him toward his dick.

Max's mouth was hot against the latex, not the same as being blown raw but good in its own way, a pleasant muted sensation. Slippery. Especially when Christian's dick slid along Max's plush lips and sank into his mouth. Christian groaned, tightening his grip on Max's hair and fucking into his mouth twice—short, abrupt strokes—before coming to his senses and pulling free again. There'd be no fucking Max at this rate. And dammit, he wasn't going to be made a liar in front of however many men were watching them now—Christian had a feeling it was a fair few more than they'd started with, judging by the stream of commentary scrolling by. Which was simultaneously terrifying and flattering. Were they here for him? For Max? For his race, for his straight act? For all of it, all mixed up in some complex chemical reaction?

Christian grabbed Max by the shoulders, turned him, and shoved him down so he was bent across his bed, ready to be fucked. Just . . . not yet. First, Christian fiddled with the camera so that Max was perfectly centered in the frame. In the meantime, Max had adjusted his position: he had his ass raised and his legs spread, so that his underwear was stretched taut around his thighs and his cock and balls hung between his legs.

The logical next step was for Christian to lube up his dick, get up behind Max, and fuck him senseless in a way that made the most skin-slapping noise. Dirty talk, groan a lot. All while keeping his face out of the frame and keeping up the pretence that he was straight.

But dammit, that wasn't what Christian *wanted*. What Christian wanted was . . .

He fell to his knees between Max's legs. The change in position put his head in the frame, but he turned his back to the camera like it didn't exist anymore.

It was just them. Him and Max. Alone.

Just their ready bodies, hot and eager and trembling. Christian reached up and hooked a finger into the waistband of Max's briefs, slowly pulling them down until they were around his ankles, the whole way caressing the muscles of Max's legs. He helped Max step out of his underwear, then guided his legs back into position.

Max himself was completely silent, even though it probably didn't make for good viewing, and Christian broke character by kissing the backs of Max's knees and murmuring against the skin of his thighs. Then he reached between Max's legs and bent back Max's cock to his mouth, suckling gently on the head until Max broke his silence with a high whine.

He tasted musky and salty, the sharp flavour of his pre-cum hitting the back of Christian's tongue. Christian had never been one for deep-throating, so he just sucked in an alternating rhythm, lips sliding over the lowest two inches of shaft. Max's hips rolled, following Christian's movements and silently begging for more, but Christian just pulled off, fisting Max's wet cock as he shifted his tongue upward to Max's taint and hole.

"Come for me," he whispered, too quiet for the camera to hear. Max keened and twisted wordlessly in reply, panting now as Christian thrust his tongue into Max's clenching hole. Not long after that, his thick cum coated Christian's fingers.

Christian rested his cheek against Max's thigh, first licking his hand clean, then stroking Max's shivering thigh with it. Waiting. Resting, until Max's body straightened and regained muscle control.

Which it did soon enough, and Max moaned "Fuck me!" theatrically, and what could Christian do but oblige him?

Standing again, he ran his hands up and down Max's sides, getting his fill of Max's dewy skin before running a perfunctorily lubed hand down his own aching shaft. "Say it again," he demanded, bellowing it out from his diaphragm.

"Fuck me!" Max repeated. "Fuck me, fuck me! Please!"

Christian *liked* the sound of that. He didn't care what that said about him.

He planted a hand on the small of Max's back and a foot on the edge of the bed, then took his cock in hand and thrust home.

Max opened up for him perfectly.

Not that Christian had expected anything less. He didn't care if it was corny: Max was *made* for him, made to complement the eccentricities of his personality and fit every inch of his body, cock and hand and lips when they kissed.

Crazy and perfect. Perfectly crazy. Christian pounded into him in long, slow strokes, then shorter, quicker, shallow ones. Grunted and groaned and half-shouted, "Take it, take it, you like that, don'tcha? Yeah." An endless stream of porno dialogue made sweet because it was for *Max*, because every moment of this mad performance brought them closer and proved once and for all that they were in this together, bound, and nothing so shallow as appearances and posturing and inadequacy would keep them apart again.

Christian rode Max's willing body until his own was ready to give out. And then he fell forward, dropping the aggressive pose so he could plaster his chest to Max's back, every inch of them touching, sharing friction and heat and desire.

"I love you," Christian cried out—who cared about their audience, who cared about the role he'd been playing, who cared about any of it at all, it was all meaningless, all appearances, all sweater-vests and superhero underwear—and then he came.

Two weeks later, Max got a six hundred dollar check in the mail.

Together, they used it to buy Auntie Beverly the biggest, brightest, most absurd bouquet of flowers that money could buy. It looked like something a Kardashian would have at their wedding, wide and tall enough that when Max held the vase in front of him, all you could see beyond the riotous red gerbera daisies and purple lilies was the very top of his head.

When they brought it through the door of Auntie Beverly's hospital room, she laughed aloud.

EPILOGUE

Three months later.

"Okay, Simon, it's time to go home now."

Simon's father stood helplessly by the door, coat in one hand and Thomas the Tank Engine backpack in the other. Meanwhile, Simon himself was doing his very best not to look at his father as he scrubbed the already-clean whiteboard with an eraser.

"*Simon*," his father repeated, an edge in his tone.

"No! I'm helping Mr. Blake! Pleeeease, Dad, just five more minutes?"

He hadn't even taken his inside shoes off yet, let alone cleaned off his desk and put up his chair like each of Christian's other twenty-four students had. The clock over the board said it was ten after three, and the classroom was empty, the school around them quiet as a church. As ready for the weekend as Christian was.

He crouched next to Simon, laying a hand on the boy's knobby shoulder. "Hey, thank you so much, but I think you've helped all you can for today, bud. What about if I put you on the chore chart for Monday to hand out the math worksheets? Would you like that?"

Simon beamed at him. "Yeah!"

"Awesome. High-five." He held up a hand and Simon gave his palm an enthusiastic smack before running to his desk and kicking out of his shoes.

A few minutes later, after waving good-bye to a cheerful Simon and his exasperated but thankful father, Christian packed up the last of his marking into his satchel to be looked at over the weekend, gave his tidy classroom one last once-over, and switched out the lights.

When he got out, Max was waiting for him at the edge of the parking lot. He greeted Christian with a peck on the lips and pushed a ragged backpack into Christian's arms.

"How was your day?" Max asked as Christian opened the bag, revealing a shiny red down vest that he quickly traded for the itchy wool argyle one he'd been wearing all day teaching.

Christian zipped up the new vest and took Max's hand, weaving their fingers together. "Pretty good, no major blowups, although there's this little girl in the third row who I think spent eighty percent of the day picking her nose. Seriously. Every time I looked up she was in to the second knuckle. No shame."

"Do you have to—I dunno, *do* something about that? Like, is that something your observing teacher is gonna give you notes on? 'Great job getting the kids to settle down for story time, but little Annie's nose picking needs to be dealt with?'"

"Uh, you know, I never thought about that?" Just one more unpredictable aspect of teaching to be added to Christian's ever-growing list. Man, all those weeks writing lesson plans and coming up with classroom management strategies, and the real question was *What do I do with a kid who's a nose picker?* "I don't think so. I guess I just gotta hope that she doesn't give herself a nosebleed or something. And make her wash her hands before snack."

Max gave their linked hands a swing, and they began their usual walk to the bus stop. Christian hadn't been sure it would work out, at first, when Max had suggested he come by every afternoon with a change of clothes. But then he remembered that he wasn't going to hide the fact that he was gay, and seeing Max on the edge of the parking lot with a change of clothes was a great, almost ritualistic, way for Christian to shift between his teacher persona and his whole self. Teacher Christian and porn-store Christian were no longer two opposing entities fighting for dominance of one body; now his sanitized teacher-self was just one part of him, as easy to put on or take off as the sweater-vest Max now had balled up in his backpack.

Now that his transformation was complete, though, they would catch the bus together, and Christian would have a nap on Max's shoulder or maybe they'd share earbuds and listen to the great new band Max had discovered that day. When they got to the store,

Christian would do the shift changeover with whoever was working days, and Max would run and pick them up supper, which they'd eat together in the store. Greek tonight—or at least, that's how Christian remembered their spirited "discussion" this morning ending; Max, on the other hand . . .

"I'm gonna run up to Hon's for Chinese," Max said when they got to the store. He pecked Christian on the cheek, flashed him a grin, and fled up the sidewalk before Christian could argue otherwise. No use going after him: Christian's shift was starting in less than two minutes, and he actually kinda liked Hon's barbeque duck. Okay, he liked it a lot. More than Greek, definitely. Huh. Maybe Max *did* know best.

He was still smiling to himself when he walked through the front door.

"*Well, well, well.* Look at you!" Auntie Beverly called from her place behind the counter. "I must admit, that boy Max dresses like a fool but I never seen you smiling so much."

"Oh my God," Christian replied, face hot with mortification. "Why do you have to say it like that?"

"Say it like what?" she asked, mischief twinkling in her eyes.

"You know full well 'like what': the whole eyebrow wiggle *thing* you just did implying like the reason I'm smiling is we just had—no, you know what, I'm not even going to say that aloud." He paced around the desk, elbowing in beside his aunt so he could clock in on the computer's system. "Your store is messing with my head. You know six months ago I'd have never even *hinted* at having a sex life around you? And now look at me, soon you're gonna be giving me suggestions on cock rings."

"I would not! I think you boys can pick out one of those by yourselves." She sniffed, primping her non-existent bob. Now that she'd finished chemo, she had a proud fuzz of black hair, which she insisted—since her doctor told her chemo often changed hair texture—would therefore grow in looking like her neighbour Yuki's. Well, stranger things *had* happened. "Now, if it's *lube* you're after, I know one—"

"Argh!" Christian cut her off, grabbed the DVD cases to be shelved, and made a beeline for the farthest corner section, where he wouldn't have to hear her anymore. Or at least, that was the plan before he stopped up short just this side of New Releases and turned on her. "And hey, what the hell are you even *doing* here, huh? Did your doctor give you permission to be back at work yet?"

"Four hours a day, I'll have you know!" she snapped, then turned from him and muttered under her breath, picking up papers and putting them down again, pretending to be busy. "Who do you think you are, anyway, the bed rest police?"

Just then, Rob appeared out of the staff bathroom, wiping something from his mouth with the back of his hand. "Nope, just the same anal-retentive stickler for the rules we've come to know and love."

"Know? Yeah, in the biblical sense. Love? Jury's still out on that one." Max swept in from the direction of the front door. He paused to kiss Auntie Beverly on the cheek before heading for Christian and enfolding him in his arms. At Christian's quizzical look, he smiled sheepishly and tilted his face up to kiss him on the chin. "So, uh, I might have forgotten I don't have a check coming in until the end of the month. I *might* need some money to cover tonight's Chinese."

"He says, two seconds after burning me for no reason." Christian reached into his back pocket, fishing out his wallet.

"C'mon, do you really blame me for taking that opening?" Max wheedled, using his growly camboy voice. "Would you still love me if I didn't?"

"Would I still love you if you weren't such a little asshole, is that what you were asking? Um, yes? The real question is, do I still love you even though you *are* a little asshole, and yes to that one, too. Ugh, I'm such an enabler." Christian rolled his eyes, then grinned. He handed Max his wallet. "Here."

"Oh, thank you, God!" Rob exclaimed, then grabbed Max by the shoulders and started shoving him toward the door. The soles of his sneakers squeaked the whole way, nearly drowning out Rob's continued complaining. "Go on, get out. If I have to hear one more second of bicker-flirting, I'm going to vomit all over both of you."

"I'll have a couple of barbeque pork buns, dear!" Aunt Beverly called, just before the door swung shut behind him.

Christian, his arms still full of foot fetish and naughty babysitter DVDs, gave a loud, exasperated sigh at the utter madness that made up his daily life. Max. Noah Hadley's Home for Wayward Gay Boys.

His aunt and her totally-not-girlfriend Sandra, who'd gone back to her usual *charming* self. Nose-picking children. Sweater-vests. Porn: both selling it and starring in it. Rear Entrance Video.

He wouldn't change a single goddamn thing.

also by **HEIDI BELLEAU**

about THE AUTHOR

Heidi Belleau was born and raised in small town New Brunswick, Canada. She now lives in the rugged oil-patch frontier of Northern BC with her husband, an Irish ex-pat whose long work hours in the trades leave her plenty of quiet time to write. She has a degree in history from Simon Fraser University with a concentration in British and Irish studies; much of her work centered on popular culture, oral folklore, and sexuality, but she was known to perplex her professors with non-ironic papers on the historical roots of modern romance novel tropes. (Ask her about Highlanders!) Her writing reflects everything she loves: diverse casts of characters, a sense of history and place, equal parts witty and filthy dialogue, the occasional mythological twist, and most of all, love—in all its weird and wonderful forms. When not writing, you might catch her trying to explain British television to her daughter or sipping a drink at her favourite coffee shop.